Daughter of Darkness

Teresa Roman

To Joanna, who's wanted to read this book from the moment I started writing it.

Thank you for your support and encouragement.

Chapter 1

Shaking and sweating, I woke up from another nightmare. Alone.

With the kind of dreams I had, I couldn't be trusted around other people while I slept. I risked hurting the people I cared about the most. And there was no way I was going to let that happen again.

After taking a few deep breaths, I threw back the covers, crawled out of bed and headed to the kitchen, where I poured myself a glass of water. As much as I needed the sleep, I knew getting back in bed would be futile, so I settled down on the couch with one of the books my cousin Rayden had given me to read: *History of the Wilds.*

I'd barely gotten through a chapter before I heard footsteps coming down the hallway. I looked up to find my cousin walking toward me.

"You couldn't sleep either?" I asked Rayden as he sat down beside me.

He shook his head. "Although not for the same reason as you."

I would've asked, but I already knew what kept him up at night. My father, Zoran. None of us liked discussing him, but that didn't keep him from being an ever-looming presence in all our lives. No one had seen or heard from him in the two weeks since he'd held me prisoner and tried to kill me, but we all knew that he hadn't just vanished. He was still out there somewhere, planning and plotting to do who knows what, and all we could do was wait for him to make his move.

"I don't want to keep living this way," I said, closing the book that rested in my lap. "I'm tired of my nightmares, and I'm tired of you and Devin and my mother worrying all the time."

"We have no other choice right now, Lilli."

I'd been hearing that ever since I left my home in Crescent City, California, to come to the Wilds. Except it wasn't true. Rayden, Devin and my mother were protecting me. They knew about my nightmares, about the way it felt like my throat was about to close every time I tried to talk about Zoran and what I'd gone through after he finally succeeded in tracking me down. That was the reason none of us had gone to the Council to report my father's crimes, because the Council would have questions—ones I wasn't ready to answer.

"I wish I knew what to do," I said, looking away, ashamed.

Rayden scooted closer to me and clasped my hands in his. "I have an idea. It's something I've been thinking about for the past few days."

"What is it?" I asked, warily.

"Keeping everything inside is doing you more harm than good. I know you're only trying to protect us, but you need to find a way to talk about what Zoran did to you."

I let out an exasperated sigh. "How am I supposed to do that?" I said, biting back the fear that came with those memories, reminding myself for the hundredth time that I had to be in control of my emotions at all times because my emotions were weapons.

"Hear me out," Rayden said calmly. "I think that once you're able to talk about what happened to you when you were in the Void with Zoran, once you're able to get it off your chest, that you'll be able to truly master your ability once and for all. And who knows, maybe you'll also stop having nightmares and get a good night's sleep for once."

I stood and turned my back to my cousin, crossing my arms. "You don't understand. It's not that I don't want to talk about what happened. It's that I can't. There's no way I can relive those things without hurting whoever I tell my story to."

I'd learned a lot about controlling my power since I'd come to find out about my unique ability, but when I got upset enough, I lost control over the fragile hold I had on my emotions. Devin had explained to me I was a reverse empath. Instead of other people's emotions affecting me, my emotions affected others. Although they didn't inflict actual physical harm, the people around me experienced them. My sadness felt like a heart being torn into pieces, my anger like a punch to the gut.

"Then don't tell a person. At least not yet. Go outside and tell your story to . . . I don't know, a tree, maybe. Pretend it's a friend or family member. Start from there and before you know it, talking about things will get easier."

Almost every night, I dreamed of demons, or of my father with his hands around my neck, choking the life out of me. Sometimes my mind wandered to those dark places even while I was awake. The idea of talking to a tree and telling it those things felt silly, but I had to do something.

I turned back around to face Rayden. "Fine," I said, dropping my arms to my sides. "I'll give it a try."

I had barely finished getting the words out before Rayden embraced me. It hadn't been that long since I'd found out that my mother, who I'd grown up thinking had died when I was a baby, was still alive, and that I had family on her side. I was still getting used to the idea, but Rayden treated me like the two of us had grown up together. "It's going to work, Lilli. You'll see."

It was still dark out. In the Wilds, there were no street lamps, so at night, the only light outside came from the moon and stars. I'd never really been afraid of the dark, but even though my cousin's cheerful outlook had bolstered me, I was still hesitant about heading outside to relive my painful memories.

After Rayden returned to his room, I grabbed my cloak from the hook beside the door, threw it on over my nightgown and headed outside. I made my way past Rayden's vegetable garden and took a few steps into the woods, staring at the trees that surrounded what had become my new home.

"Here goes nothing," I said. I took a deep breath and closed my eyes for a moment before plunging into my story.

At first, I felt silly, pouring my heart out to no one in particular, but after a while, the words just flowed. As I spoke, a chill ran through me. I pulled the cloak I wore tighter around my body. When I got to the part about Zoran summoning Andras, tears began to stream down my face. I choked on my words more than once, but I kept going, pushing through until the end.

When I was done with my story, I fell to my knees and wrapped my arms around my body. I fought back against the despair that threatened to consume me, as the most heartbreaking moment of my life flashed through my mind—the moment I learned that Zoran was my father, not the man who had raised me. Sobbing, I lay down and curled into a ball. For weeks, I'd slept fitfully, and it had finally caught up to me. I lay there, exhausted and willing myself to get up and go back inside, but instead I fell fast asleep right there on the cold, hard earth.

When I awoke, light had already begun to stream over the horizon. I sat up and realized with horror that the earth below me was scorched. I must have done that during the night while reliving my memories. It had been too dark for me to notice it then, and I was too wrapped up in my pain. At least I hadn't harmed anyone, I told myself.

"Lilli, Lilli?"

Still groggy, it took me a moment to realize that my name was being called. I stood. "I'm out here, in the back," I shouted.

A moment later, Rayden walked up to me. "Have you been out here since we talked?"

I wiped the dirt from my cloak. "I took your advice, but after I was done getting everything off my chest, I felt so tired, so I lay down and somehow I just fell asleep."

"Are you okay?" Rayden's eyes flitted back and forth between me and the ground where I'd been lying.

I hesitated before answering him. "Yes." I smiled feebly as it sunk in that Rayden had been right. It was as if I'd been ill for weeks and my fever had finally broken. The memories I'd tried to bottle no longer seemed to hold the same power over me. "I'm okay," I said, silently praying that my newfound confidence would last.

Like he did every morning, Devin came over a few hours later. I was in the middle of washing a tub full of breakfast dishes when he walked over to me, snaked his arms around my waist, and planted a kiss on the nape of my neck.

"Good morning, my beautiful flower," he whispered into my ear.

I never tired of the way he greeted me. With still-soapy hands, I turned around and looked into his eyes, their blue-green color reminding me of the ocean. I wiped my hands on my apron and then kissed him back while running one of my hands through his wavy chestnut hair.

Rayden cleared his throat. "Just thought I'd let the two of you know that I'm heading to my shop."

My cousin was a healer and owned an apothecary that sold all kinds of medicinal herbs. I had yet to visit it, even though it's where Rayden spent most of his days. Since arriving in the Wilds, the only places I spent time in (other than my cousin's house) was the woods surrounding it, and my mother's home. Devin and my mother had warned me that going into town meant facing stares and whispers. I looked so much like my mother— same long dark hair, gray eyes and pale complexion—that people would recognize me, and they'd ask questions, ones I wasn't prepared to answer. And word would reach the Council that Naiara had a daughter, a daughter no one knew existed until recently. But I was beginning to get cabin fever. I couldn't hide from the world forever.

I was about to wish my cousin a good day when I felt Devin's broad shoulders stiffen.

"What's wrong?" I asked.

"Someone's coming."

He took a step back from me and stared at the door. "Lilli, go into the bedroom."

"Is it Zoran?"

"No." Being half shape-shifter meant Devin's senses were so sharp that, if Zoran were standing outside the door, Devin could recognize his scent. "But I don't want whoever Rayden's visitor is seeing you until I know if they are a friend or foe."

A knock sounded on the door, and I rushed down the hall and into my room, leaving the door open a crack so I could hear what was about to be said.

A moment later, I heard Devin and Rayden greeting a man who introduced himself as Byron.

"What brings a Messenger to my home?" Rayden asked.

"The Council has some questions for you."

"What would the Council possibly want from me?" Rayden sounded convincingly curious.

"Zoran Raeburn has been missing for over two weeks. Since you are his wife's cousin, the Council is hoping you may be able to help them find him."

"Have you spoken to Naiara yet?"

"She has already been summoned to the Council's compound," Byron replied. "Once I arrive with you, the questioning can begin."

"Well, I don't know where Zoran is. And I've got to get to my shop, so you can let the Council know that sending you here was a waste of time."

"That's not how this works," Byron said. "You are to come

with me and answer whatever questions the Council sees fit to ask you. And I will remind you, just as I reminded Naiara, that there is no use lying to them. They will know if you aren't being truthful."

"This is a waste of time," Rayden said angrily.

"Does he have to come right now?" Devin asked. "Can't you let him arrange to have someone take care of his shop first?"

There was still so much for me to learn about the Wilds and magic and everything else, but I knew enough to realize there was no way Devin or Rayden was going to convince Byron to back down. If anything, they'd just get themselves in trouble if they kept trying. The Council and their Messengers had been in power for hundreds of years. They wouldn't have stayed that way if they let people disobey.

"I'm getting the feeling that you two are hiding something."

"What would we possibly have to hide?" Rayden scoffed. "I just don't appreciate being asked to drop everything when I have no answers to give about what happened to Zoran."

I knew what Devin and my cousin were trying to do. They were trying to keep me a secret until they were sure I was ready to talk about the terrible things my father had done. But the Council had already summoned my mother, so it wouldn't be long before they learned about me from her and dragged me in for questioning.

"If that's truly the case, then this shouldn't take long," Byron said. "Now give me your hand."

I pushed my bedroom door open and hurried down the hallway before I lost my nerve.

Devin saw me first. He ran over to me, trying to use his body to block mine from view. "What are you doing?" he whispered.

I stepped around him. "If the Council has questions for my mother and my cousin, then I'm sure they will have some for me as well."

Byron's eyes, which he'd just closed in preparation for teleporting, flicked open at the sound of my voice. He dropped Rayden's hand and stared at me with his eyebrows raised. "You can't possibly be who I think you are."

"I . . . I'm Lilli—"

"You look so much like . . . Naiara," Byron said, staring. "It's uncanny."

"Lilli, what are you doing?" Rayden said.

"What I should have done a long time ago."

Byron extended his hand. "You will need to come with me."

I walked over to him, taking his hand.

"Wait," Devin said. His eyes darted back and forth between Byron and me as if he were trying to figure out what to do. "If you're taking both of them with you, I might as well come along, too, because I've also got information the Council needs to hear."

"Hmmm," Byron grunted. "I don't doubt that's true."

Devin took my other hand; the one Byron wasn't clenching. "What were you thinking?" he whispered in my ear.

"That I'm tired of hiding." I sounded a lot braver than I actually felt.

"Close your eyes," Byron commanded. With a thundering heart, I did as I was told, anticipating not only the sensations that came with transporting yourself from one place to the next with magic, but wondering what I would see moments from now when I opened my eyes again.

Chapter 2

Teleportation was the main means of transport used by witches. It was easy enough to do. Witches simply had to close their eyes and picture where they wanted to go, and moments later, that's exactly where they'd be. At first, it had been a dizzying experience, but over time, teleporting had begun to feel more like floating through the air. Still an odd sensation, but tolerable. It was an amazing thing to be in one place and, a moment later, in another. There were limitations to teleporting, though. Witches' homes in the Wilds were magically warded so people couldn't just appear inside your house. And teleporting to a place one had never been to before was, while not impossible, trickier. There was no guarantee you'd wind up where you planned to.

But even if I had been to the Council's compound before, none of us could teleport there without Byron's help, which was why he had us link hands. Devin had explained once that the Council had all sorts of protection spells in place to keep themselves safe from the constant threat that came from those who wanted them removed as the guardians of the Wilds.

When I opened my eyes a few seconds after Byron and Devin

had taken my hands, I found that we were standing in a large grassy field. Off in the distance in one direction lay craggy rock, the kind you saw at the edges of cliffs. In the other, a thick, dense forest. It truly looked like we were in the middle of nowhere. This was hardly the first time I'd felt that way since coming to the Wilds. Walking through the woods around Rayden's and my mother's homes left me with that same middle-of-nowhere feeling I now had.

Much closer than either the forest behind me or the cliff in front of me, only a few feet away, was the Council's compound, which was square-shaped, but with three sides instead of four. Inside the square was a courtyard paved in the same gray-brown concrete. At each outer corner of the courtyard stood two identical statues on pedestals. They looked like some sort of mythical creatures—half lion, half bird. Small windows dotted the sides of the building. In the center of each side of the compound were gigantic doors made of thick wooden planks.

Despite the strangeness of my surroundings, something seemed familiar. It took me a moment to realize why. I'd seen this exact place before in my dreams. This was the place I'd seen when only a month or so ago I'd dreamed of Zoran's father being murdered. Only a few feet away from where I now stood, Zoran's mother had struggled to protect her son, who was only a small child at the time, while demons, appearing out of nowhere, had slaughtered her husband.

I still remembered the terror I felt watching that scene unfold in front of me, and how I'd awakened from my sleep trembling. Ever since I was a little girl, I'd had frightening dreams of demons and witches, but it wasn't until a few months ago that I learned my dreams were of things that had actually happened, not the workings of a disturbed child's mind.

Devin, Rayden and I followed Byron into the courtyard where seven chairs and a large wooden table with elaborate carvings were set up. Right across from that table sat my mother, whose head turned as we approached. Her already-pale face blanched at the sight of me.

She stood. "Please, Byron, leave my daughter out of this. She has been through so much. Whatever answers the Council seeks, I can be the one to give them."

"That isn't up for me to decide," he replied coldly before waving a hand through the air. A moment later, a chair appeared beside my mother's. He waved his hand two more times, and each time he did, another chair appeared. My jaw dropped.

"It's called conjuring," Devin whispered into my ear.

I furrowed my brows. "So he can just make anything appear out of nowhere?"

"Not exactly. The Council puts strict limits on conjuring."

Hesitantly, I sat down between Devin and my mother, who still looked ashen. Rayden took the last empty chair. Without another word, Byron walked away, disappearing behind one of the doors to the compound.

"He doesn't seem very friendly," I said of Byron.

"They do not care for our approval or for friendship," my mother said in such a quiet voice that I barely heard her. "Only our respect."

"That seems like a lonely way to live," I replied.

"I think they get used to it. And though they spend most of their time up here, away from others, they have each other for company," Rayden explained.

"Unlike the Council, Messengers at least are allowed to marry and have children," my mother added, "but you're right, they sacrifice a lot when they accept their positions. Because they know that without them, witchkind would be lost."

"You must be nervous, but there's no need to be," Devin said, gripping my hand a little tighter. "All we have to do is tell the Council the truth. They'll understand."

"What if they don't believe us?"

"It is not a question of belief," my mother said.

"What does that mean?" It was a question I'd often had to ask since coming to the Wilds, a place that I never even knew existed until recently when Devin had explained that the human world I'd lived in all my life wasn't the only one that existed. The Wilds was where witches lived, just like the Underworld was home to demons and Faerie was home to the fae.

"One of the seven members of the Council possesses the ability to know when they are being lied to," she replied.

"Which is a good thing," Devin explained, "because now that we have hard facts instead of mere speculation or suspicions, the Council will have no choice but to act for the good of all witchkind."

I remembered asking him once, while the two of us were on the run, hiding from the tracker demons that Zoran had sent to bring me to him, why no one had gone to the Council to tell them how evil Zoran was. Without proof, Devin had said, the Council wouldn't believe him or me or anyone else. They had a soft spot when it came to Zoran, one that blinded them from seeing who he really was. Zoran's father had been a Messenger. After he died, his mother fell into such a deep state of grief that she was unable to care for her son. The Council took him under their wing, raising him as if he were their adopted child.

But after I presented the Council with the pile of evidence I now had, they would have no choice but to see the truth—that Zoran was a power-hungry witch who would stop at nothing to get what he wanted. At least that's what I tried convincing myself of as we sat there waiting for them to emerge from their compound.

"Lilli, are you sure you're ready for this?" my mother asked.

I looked at her, feeling terrible about the worry etched on her face. "I . . . I think I am."

"I don't want you to worry about us," Devin said to me. "Whatever happens, we'll be fine. Just answer the Council's questions the best you can."

With each second that ticked by, I became more nervous, remembering how badly I'd hurt Devin without meaning to after he and my mother had stopped Zoran from killing me. When I'd shown myself to Byron, I had been so much surer of myself, but my doubts grew by the second. When the door directly in front of us opened, my heart hammered in my chest. I told myself that the sooner we got this over with, the better. Still, I couldn't help but worry about telling my story to seven strangers, especially since it would be the first time my family and Devin heard it.

One by one, seven people who wore dark cloaks with hoods that hid their faces streamed out onto the courtyard. They stood behind their chairs, waiting until the door to the compound closed before sitting and pulling their hoods back.

The man seated in the middle spoke first. "It appears that Byron was correct." He directed his gaze toward me. "We are about to hear quite the story."

Chapter 3

"Before we begin, let us introduce ourselves." The man seated in the middle chair stood. "I am Syre, eldest member of the Council of Witches."

I wondered if being the eldest meant that he was in charge. He looked the part. His neatly trimmed white beard gave him a wise-old-man appearance and he carried an air of authority.

One by one, each Council member stood and introduced himself or herself in the same monotone voice. When the introductions were completed, they all sat down again. Silently, I repeated their names, trying to keep them straight. Beside Syre on the left sat Alonzo, Sana and Ina, on his right Troy, Marus and Tressa.

"You're going to be fine," Devin whispered, sensing my unease.

For a moment, I wondered if I was also supposed to introduce myself, but then Syre spoke again. "It is a pleasure to meet you, Lilli Raeburn."

"I . . . don't go by that name. I'm Lilli Young."

Syre furrowed his brows in confusion. "May I ask, to whom does that surname belong?"

"It was my father's last name." I clenched my hands together in my lap. "I mean, the man who raised me. He wasn't my real father, but I didn't know that until a few weeks ago."

Syre leaned back in his chair. "We're getting ahead of ourselves," he said in a calm voice. "Let us start at the beginning."

"Um," I said, trying to figure out where the beginning of my story actually was. "I'm not sure what exactly you all want to know."

"How old are you, child?" asked Marus.

"Eighteen."

He frowned. "Where have you been for all of those years?"

"In California," I replied, not sure if any of them knew where that was.

"Your daughter was raised in the human world?" Sana addressed my mother, her tone sharp.

Before she could reply, Syre spoke. "We will save our questions for Naiara until her daughter finishes her story." He paused before continuing, addressing me this time. "Tell us how, after all these years, you wound up here."

I took a deep breath. "Well, it all started after my father died. His name was Mark Young, and he was the only parent I knew until a few months ago when he had a heart attack." I wondered if the Council knew what that was. Did witches have heart attacks? Instead of explaining, I pressed on, figuring if they didn't, someone would've interrupted. "During his funeral, I saw my mother at the cemetery. Except, at the time, I didn't know it was actually her. I thought it was her ghost, which would be weird for most people, but not for me, because ever since I was a little girl I've seen strange things. And I had the craziest dreams, too, but I was scared to talk about them because I worried people would think I was nuts. But it's hard keeping so much to yourself all the time, and after my dad died I had no one to tell my secrets to, so I confided in Devin." I glanced at him. "I should've been suspicious when he told me he didn't think I was crazy."

"Tell me how it was that the two of you crossed paths," Tressa said.

"Um, we met at a coffee shop. I was looking for a job, and Devin helped me find one."

"What were you doing at a coffee shop in the human world?" Alonzo asked, addressing Devin.

Before Devin could answer, Syre cut him off. "Please direct your questions to Lilli. Devin's turn to speak is coming." He turned his attention back to me. "Continue," he commanded.

"I was still grieving over my father's death, which was why Devin didn't tell me about being a witch and the Wilds and my mother still being alive sooner. I guess he wanted to wait until he thought I was ready to hear the truth. But somehow, I just knew that he was keeping something from me, so I kept bugging him until he finally told me everything."

"Everything?" Marus asked with a raised brow.

"Well, as much as he knew."

"Which was what?" Ina asked.

"That my mother was alive and well and a witch who lived in a place called the Wilds, a world humans don't know exists."

"You must have been very curious about what it was like here," Syre mused.

"I was. But Devin said it wasn't safe for me to come here. Back then, we both assumed I was half-human and that the man who raised me really was my father. That meant if Zoran ever found out about me, I'd be in danger. Devin figured that had to be the reason my mother left me in the human world," I said, shifting in my chair. "Even though that seemed to make sense, I couldn't stop wondering if he was right. I had so many questions for my mother that I begged Devin to bring me here so I could ask them. At first he said it was too dangerous, but I wouldn't listen, and eventually Devin gave in and agreed to help arrange for me to meet my mother. We were only here for a short time, less than a day, but it was enough time for me to meet my mother and Rayden and . . . for Zoran to find out about me."

"How do you know he found out?" Troy asked.

"Because not long after Devin and I returned home, Zoran sent a tracker demon to look for me. Devin was able to . . . to destroy it, but he said more would come, and if we didn't hide, the next time one appeared, we wouldn't be so lucky. So the two of us went on the run. We drove halfway across the country, trying to keep Zoran from finding me, but he had other witches helping him. One of them went to my Aunt Kate's house looking for me, and he made her call me. He told me he'd hurt her if I didn't tell him where I was."

"What was this witch's name?" Syre asked.

"Sabin."

Several of the Council members shifted uneasily in their seats.

"So, you told Sabin how to find you? What happened then?"

"He brought me to a place called the Void. Although I didn't know that's where we were at first; I thought I was just in some cave." The Void, I'd later come to learn, was some sort of no man's land in between worlds. "That was where I met Zoran for the first time." My voice trembled as I remembered the fear I felt then. I took a deep breath and closed my eyes, pushing the memory of Zoran's angry face out of my mind and filling it with calmer thoughts just like my mother had taught me to do.

"What happened then?" Ina asked impatiently.

"I thought he was going to kill me," I said. "He wanted me gone, he said, because there was no way he could accept that my mother had a child with another man. But he'd decided that instead of killing me, he'd use me as a bargaining chip. You see, once Zoran learned that my mother had loved someone else and had a child with that man, he became obsessed with the fact that playing by the rules hadn't gotten him anywhere. He wanted my mother to be his and his alone and he'd wanted a child with her. And neither of those things happened. He was angry, and said it was your rules that kept him from having the life he wanted. So he decided to do something about it by striking a bargain with a powerful demon named Andras."

The faces of the Council members paled, and they exchanged furtive glances, but they remained silent and let me continue talking.

"He had two other witches help him summon the demon. Sabin and . . . and Kees." I hadn't wanted to mention Kees, because he'd tried to help me, and I felt like I owed him for that, but I figured the Council would ask for his name and I'd have no choice but to give it to them. "Although Kees didn't want to help Zoran, he only did because he had no other option. Zoran would've killed him if he hadn't."

"What did Zoran want from Andras?" Alonzo asked.

"He wanted his help. He wanted to learn enough dark magic

so he could get rid of all of you." I paused just long enough to swallow the lump that had formed in my throat. "Demons demand a price, though, so Zoran offered me in exchange as a bride to Andras."

I glanced at Devin who was gripping the arms of his chair tightly, his face like stone. I regretted that I hadn't had the courage to tell him about Andras sooner, and in private. This wasn't the way I'd wanted him to hear about it.

"The girl lies," Marus said angrily. "The Zoran she is describing is not the one we all know. I don't know how she's doing it, but this story cannot be true."

Devin jumped to his feet. "Lilli is not a liar."

"Quiet!" Marus roared. "You will not speak until you are asked to."

Marus wasn't the only one outraged. Devin's jaw was clenched, and his hands were curled into fists. I wasn't sure what had upset him more: Marus accusing me of lying, or what I'd just said about Zoran offering me as a bride to a demon.

"That's enough." Syre's voice boomed like thunder. "Let the girl finish her story. We can deliberate the merits of it after all our questions have been answered." He turned his gaze toward me once more. "Go on. Tell us what happened next."

"Andras refused to make a bargain with Zoran," I said, leaving out the part about how disgusted and frightened I'd been as Andras touched me and how out of nowhere he'd fallen to the ground, writhing in pain from the power I hadn't yet realized I had. "Zoran blamed me. He was so angry, and said if Andras didn't want me, then he had no use for me. He put his hands around my neck and started to choke me. I thought for sure he'd kill me, but somehow Devin and my mother managed to find me before he could.

"My mother begged him to leave me alone, but Zoran was too angry to care about what she wanted. He tried to choke me again, right in front of her. That's when she told him that I was his daughter—"

Another knot formed in my throat. Focus, I told myself. Keep your feelings wrapped around you. For the past two weeks, Devin and my mother had been trying to teach me how to control my power. I'd learned to meditate and focus. By sheer will, I kept people safe from the effects of my emotions, but it was so much harder to do when I became overwhelmed. I looked to my right where Rayden and my mother sat, then to my left at Devin. I would not hurt them. I would not hurt them. With steely determination, I managed to detach myself and continued my story as if I were talking about things that had happened to someone else.

"I refused to believe I was his daughter at first, but somewhere inside I knew she wasn't lying, and I became so angry and so . . . sad at the same time. It hadn't been that long since Mark was buried"—it felt strange calling him by his name instead of Dad—"and I loved him so much. He was a good man, not like Zoran, who is filled with evil. I hated that his blood ran through my veins, that the man who tried to give me to a demon, the man who tried to choke me to death, was my father. I became so full of the darkest, ugliest feelings that I didn't realize what was happening at first."

A look of recognition crossed Syre's face. "A reverse empath," he said in a quiet voice before turning his head first to the left, then the right, then back to me. "Is that why you've been hiding from us all this time, because you were afraid to speak?"

I nodded. How he'd just figured that out, I had no idea. He was either telepathic or extremely adept at reading people.

"But you managed to control your power just now. Even though it's only been . . . how long since you learned you had it?"

"Two weeks."

"That is extraordinary."

"My mother and Devin have been helping me."

"Still, it must've taken a great deal of focus and strength of will to tell us what you just did."

"Yes," I said, realizing suddenly how completely drained I felt. "It did."

"Then we are all the more grateful to you." A few other Council members nodded their heads in agreement. The rest sat there, staring at me, steely-faced.

Syre snapped his fingers, and a few seconds later, the door to the compound behind him opened. When a hooded figure stepped out, Syre beckoned. It was a woman this time, I realized, as she pulled back the hood of her cloak. Syre whispered something to her.

She approached me with her hands clasped behind her back. "Come."

"Where are you taking her?" Devin asked. He looked like he was restraining himself from springing out of his chair again.

"Home," the Messenger said softly and in a gentle voice. "The rest of you can follow her there when the Council is done questioning you."

"She's not going anywhere without me."

"The girl is exhausted, Devin," Syre said. "You have no idea the energy it takes for her to restrain so many strong emotions. Let her return home to rest."

"She'll be fine, Devin," my mother said.

I wasn't sure why, but I trusted Syre and the Messenger. I stood and followed her, looking over my shoulder to see that my mother, Rayden and Devin all had their heads turned, watching me as I walked away. I could tell by the expression on Devin's face that he was using every last ounce of self-control he had to keep himself from running after me. Rayden and my mother also looked distressed. They were all shocked by the story I'd just shared. It suddenly occurred to me that there was something I could do to help.

I thought about the many times Devin had comforted me and reassured me when I'd been frightened. Not wanting any of them to worry, I pictured myself grabbing ahold of that contented feeling and casting it out like a net, spreading it over them so they would feel it, too.

The Messenger continued to lead me into the grassy field that surrounded the compound. "My name is Lina," she finally said. "And I have been tasked with two things. The first is to take you home. The second is"—she reached into her pocket—"to give you this." She handed me an amulet.

"What is it for?" I asked, taking it from her hand.

"Wear it around your neck. It is the fastest way to summon one of us in case you need help, or in case you have any more information the Council needs to hear. All you have to do is hold the amulet in the palm of your hand while chanting this incantation:

Peril stands before my eyes. Find me now so I may testify.

The chain the amulet hung from was long, enabling me to slip it over my head.

"Repeat the words, so I know you've learned them."

After I did, Lina said, "The Council doesn't just hand these out to anyone, child, so use it wisely."

She grasped my hand, and I closed my eyes, realizing she meant to return me home. When I opened them, the two of us stood a few feet away from the door to Rayden's house. Lina turned to me, bowed, and then vanished without uttering a single word.

I walked inside with a surprising sense of relief. I sat down on the couch waiting for Devin, Rayden and my mother to return, praying that when they did, they'd tell me the Council had believed me and that they would do whatever they could to find Zoran. As I sat there, I fingered the amulet around my neck, an oval, deep-blue stone, and hoped I'd never have to use it.

When Devin had asked me to come to the Wilds with him, I agreed because I wanted to be with him, and this was his home. But I'd also agreed because I wanted to get to know the family I never knew I had better. This was not only Devin's home, it was where his family lived, and where mine did, too, so agreeing to come seemed like the only logical choice. Despite how different and strange things were, I was awed by this magical world, and sure I could be happy here, we could be happy here. But not until Council captured my father.

Chapter 4

The hands of the clock on the mantle above the fireplace moved painfully slow as time ticked by. I wanted to get the rest that Syre had somehow known I needed, but the relief I'd felt earlier had turned into worry as I thought about the expression on Devin's face when I'd told the Council my story. I also couldn't help but think about the way Marus had accused me of lying. What if the Council didn't believe me? They had to, I told myself. Hadn't my mother said that one of them possessed the ability to know when they were being lied to? Every word I'd uttered had been the truth, whether they liked it or not.

Almost an hour passed before Rayden, Devin and my mother returned. I jumped to my feet as soon as they walked inside the house.

"Tell me what happened," I said. "What other questions did the Council ask?"

My mother opened her mouth to speak, but Devin cut her off. "We can talk about that later." He took a step closer to me and grasped my arms.

I looked into his eyes, which were as serious as I'd ever seen them. "Later? Why?"

"Because I want to discuss something with you first, privately."

"Devin," my mother said, reaching for him. "Perhaps now isn't the right time."

"Naiara, that should be up to the two of them to decide," Rayden said.

"Okay," I said, still staring into Devin's eyes. "Do you want to go to my room or should we take a walk?"

"Neither, actually. There's somewhere I've been meaning to take you to since you arrived here."

I furrowed my brows in confusion. He'd never mentioned this place before. "Where?"

"Close your eyes." When I hesitated, he said, "Trust me."

So I did. A few seconds later, we were standing in the middle of a grassy field. There was not another soul around, even though the beauty of my surroundings almost begged for visitors to admire its magnificence. The meadow where we stood was split in half by a dirt path that led toward both forest and mountains in the distance and was dotted with large, weeping trees whose branches hung so low that if you stood under their shelter, you'd most certainly be obscured from view. I took in a deep breath, appreciating the fresh air and the scent of grass.

"Come." Devin pulled my hand, and I followed him as he found a place for us to sit at the foot of a tree. The sun was high in the sky, but under the shade of the tree, the heat was tolerable, especially when a breeze swept through the air.

"Where exactly are we?"

"At the foot of the Black Hills," he said, pointing to them off in the distance.

I hadn't understood why the Wilds was called what it was

until Devin had brought me. It was such an apt description. All I'd seen since I'd gotten here was a place unsullied by modern technology. No cars or roads, no neon signs or traffic lights. It felt like I'd gone back in time. Blue skies, green grass, brown earth. The woods around Rayden's and my mother's homes seemed as endless as the field I now sat in. This particular place reminded me of the opening scene from *The Sound of Music*, one of my father's favorite classic movies. For a moment I thought about spinning around to get a better view of my surroundings.

"It's so beautiful . . . and quiet."

"Yes, it is, which is why I come here whenever I need to think."

"So what is it you want to talk about?" I asked, fairly sure I already knew the answer.

"It was brave of you to tell the Council what happened when you were in the Void with Zoran," he said, tucking my hair behind one of my ears. "You have done an amazing job learning to control your ability."

"Thanks to you and my mother. And Rayden," I added, remembering it was Rayden's advice in the dead of night that had helped me deal with the burden of my memories.

Devin looked away and bowed his head.

"What's wrong?" I asked, putting my hand on his knee.

"I've failed you, Lilli. Time and time again. I swore I'd protect you from Zoran, but he managed to get to you anyway. I knew he'd done bad things to you in the Void, but offering you up to a demon . . ." he shook his head. "I can't even begin to imagine how frightening that must've been."

"It was." I shuddered inside at the memory of Andras's coal-black eyes and the way he smelled of ash. "But none of that was your fault."

Devin lifted his head and stared at me without saying a word. The color had drained from his face. Tension filled the air, building with every second of passing silence, until I couldn't stand it anymore.

"Say something," I whispered.

Without a word Devin stood and walked a few paces away while I just sat there, staring at his back, unsure of what to do. A moment later, he stopped at a large limb that had fallen from a tree a few yards away. He picked it up and lifted it over his head with superhuman strength.

"I'll kill him *and* that demon he tried to hand you over to," he shouted, his voice echoing as he hurled the tree limb across the field. "I'll kill them both."

I ran to Devin and wrapped my arms around him, wanting at the same time to comfort him and be comforted by him.

"How could you love me after I let that happen to you?" Devin finally said.

I broke my embrace to put a hand under Devin's chin, lifting his bowed head so he could look into my eyes. "You didn't *let* anything happen to me. One way or another Zoran would have found me. He was determined, and nothing either one of us could have done would've stopped him."

He shook his head. "I don't deserve you."

"Devin, you have to listen to me. What happened to me was destined. My mother had a vision before I was even born that one day my father would try to kill me." Devin knew that my mother was a seer, but I hadn't told him the story she'd shared with me after I'd managed to escape the Void and find my way back home. "It was the reason she ran away from here and the reason she left me behind in Crescent City. But in spite of every sacrifice she made, Zoran was able to find me anyway."

Devin reached for my hands, twining his fingers through mine. "Just tell me one thing. Did he lay a hand on you? That filthy demon, did he touch you?" Anger simmered beneath Devin's calm façade. I knew if I told him about the way Andras had touched me, that he'd almost kissed me, it would send Devin over the edge.

"No." I shook my head. "I was really scared, and even though I didn't realize what I was doing then, I made Andras feel my fear. It brought him to his knees."

Devin's eyes fluttered shut for a moment. "Thank the worlds for that."

"Zoran was furious. He wanted to know what I'd done to Andras, but I didn't know myself. With Andras gone, Zoran said he had no use for me, which is why he had his hands around my neck when you and my mother found me."

"I don't know what to do," Devin said, releasing my hands and then clenching his into fists. "I want to go and find Zoran myself and plunge a dagger into his chest where his heart should be. Damn what the Council thinks."

"No one knows where he is, and even if you could find him, do you really think he's going to let you get close enough to him to do that?"

My father was a powerful telekinetic. In the blink of an eye he'd have Devin flying through the air.

"No, he won't," Devin agreed. "Which means I won't use a

dagger then. An arrow will work just as well. My sharp senses make me an expert marksman."

Devin's enhanced senses weren't magical in the same way my ability was. They were a product of his mixed heritage. His mother was a witch, his birth father a shape-shifter.

"He's my father," I said, even though, truthfully, I didn't care about that. Father or not, I'd spent enough time around him to know that where his heart should be there was nothing but darkness. I didn't want Devin trying to track Zoran down. It was too dangerous, and I had no idea how I'd survive if anything ever happened to him.

"He doesn't deserve your loyalty, Lilli, even if he is your father."

"I'm not loyal to Zoran. I just think the further we both stay away from him, the better. Let the Council deal with him. Let them give Zoran the punishment he deserves."

Devin's jaw twitched. "Right now I don't care about justice. I want *revenge*."

"When Zoran held me prisoner I was sure I'd never see you again. I can't go through that again. Which is why I'm asking you to leave Zoran to the Council. We deserve some peace."

Devin closed his eyes for a moment. "I'm sorry." He put his arms around me and pulled me closer. My heart quickened at his touch. "I shouldn't be talking like this. I'm supposed to be the one making you feel better, not the other way around."

"I'm always better when you're with me," I said, resting my head on his chest.

Just being around Devin made me feel warm and content. It had been that way since we first met. But no matter how badly I clung to the hope that the peace I felt in Devin's arms would never end, as we stood there, I couldn't help but worry that one day it would.

Chapter 5

It was too beautiful outside to return home right away, so Devin and I took a walk instead. I was afraid to ask more questions about the Council. For a while neither of us said a word to each other. Eventually my curiosity got the better of me.

"What happened after I left? Did the Council believe my story?"

"They might not have wanted to, but they really had no other choice. Marus tried convincing everyone else that you had some sort of power to trick them, but Syre told him to stop being foolish, that it was time they all stopped being so blind when it came to Zoran."

His words made it feel like a weight had been lifted off my shoulders. "What else did they say?"

Devin sighed. "Your mother, Rayden and I got an earful about how many rules we broke. But the Council did give us a chance to explain why we all did what we did."

"They understood, right?" I asked hopefully.

Devin frowned. "I wouldn't say that, exactly."

"Out with it already. What did they tell you?"

Devin stopped walking and turned to me, taking my hands in his. "That luckily for us, they have bigger things to worry about than how many rules we broke."

Relief washed over me. My mother had explained to me the kind of punishment Devin, Rayden and especially she risked getting once the Council found out about me. Witches had been banished from the Wilds, their memories stripped, for lesser offenses. "That's a good thing, isn't it?"

"Yes and no." We started walking again. "I'm glad the Council decided not to punish us, but I'm worried about how afraid they seem. They usually come down much harder on people who did what we did."

"Maybe they just understood your reasons."

Devin shook his head. "We risked exposing magic to humans. That's not something the Council takes lightly, no matter the reasons. You've been reading *The History of the Wilds*. You know what happened to our kind when we lived amongst humans. A lot of innocent blood was shed."

I remembered reading all about that in the book Rayden had given me. Hundreds of years ago witches and humans lived amongst each other. For many years humans appreciated the talents of my ancestors. They turned to witches for healing and love potions, and all sorts of other things magic helped them with. But then humans began to fear witches; they didn't trust us because of our powers. Witches started hiding their abilities from humans, and did their best to blend in. But that only made humans even more suspicious. They started accusing people of witchcraft, arrested them and put them on trial. Many of the accused weren't witches at all, and without magic to aid them, they faced horrible deaths. Some were hanged, others burned at the stake. That was when witches decided to separate themselves from humankind for good and escaped back into the Wilds, a magical world beyond human reach.

"That was such a long time ago. Things have changed. Nobody gets burned at the stake anymore."

Devin glanced at me and offered a weak smile. "Enough about the Council. It's getting late, perhaps we should return home. I'm sure your mother and Rayden are just as anxious to speak with you as I was."

I hesitated. It was so peaceful out here that I wanted to stay a bit longer, but he was right, so I took his hand and closed my eyes. When we got back to Rayden's, he was sitting with my mother at the table, drinking tea. I'd never been much of a tea drinker, but in the Wilds, people drank it all the time. Not only with meals, either. Rayden's kettle was always full of hot water, ready to be poured into a cup, along with leaves for brewing. There were bitter teas and sweet teas, teas to warm you up, and others to calm the nerves.

I didn't ask him what kind he'd made as he poured a cup for Devin and me.

"So what were you two talking about before we got here?" Devin asked after taking a sip.

"I was just telling Naiara that she and Lilli are the Council's best chance of finding Zoran."

My mother shook her head. "You are mistaken if you think my missing husband will suddenly reappear and share his whereabouts with me," she said.

"If he makes contact with anyone, it will either be with you or with Lilli," Rayden replied, sounding sure of himself.

The thought sent a chill down my spine. I didn't even want to think about coming face to face with him again. "What do you think will happen to Zoran when the Council finds him?"

"I imagine he'll be stripped of his powers and sent to Bloodstone Island," my mother said.

"It's a prison, like that place in the human world, Alcatraz," Devin explained "No one has ever escaped. The waters surrounding the island are filled with kelpies and selkies looking for their next victims."

"The Council will have to catch Zoran first," Rayden said, "I suspect that won't be an easy thing to do."

"They will," Devin said, sounding certain.

"You're being overly optimistic, my friend. And I think I know why. But Lilli should know the truth. You can't sugarcoat things for her all the time. She's tougher than you think she is."

I looked back and forth between Rayden and Devin. "What are you guys not telling me?"

"We don't know anything for sure," Rayden answered. "But if Zoran turned to Andras, who's to say he isn't looking for some other demon to help him achieve his goals? Maybe even more than one."

"I can't believe Zoran could have anything but hate in his heart for demons after what happened to his father," I said.

"They are but a means to an end," Rayden explained. "And at this point, Zoran doesn't have many choices. He either has to move forward with whatever he was planning to do or wait for the Council to find him and hand out his punishment. I don't picture him doing that."

"Just because Zoran isn't cowering in some corner doesn't mean he's going to get away with what he's done," Devin said.

"I'm not saying he will," Rayden replied. "But we shouldn't fool ourselves into thinking this will be easy, that the Council will just find Zoran soon, and our problems will all of a sudden be over."

"This is my fault," I said, cutting into their conversation. "I should've gone to the Council right away instead of waiting for them to come to us."

Devin rested his hand on top of mine. "You weren't in any condition to—"

"I know," I said. "But I should've been. I should've been stronger."

"No one expected you to be, Lilli," Rayden said. "If anything, we're all amazed at how quickly you were able to master your ability."

"Enough already about Zoran and the Council," my mother said, standing from the table with what looked like a forced smile on her face. "What we all need right now is a nice dinner to take our minds off this most trying day. I expect to see you all at my house in an hour. That should be all the time I need."

She vanished without waiting for our reply. We sat there for a few moments without saying a word.

"Speaking of family dinners," Devin said, breaking the silence. "I was hoping we could have one of our own soon. My parents and my brother have been eager to meet you."

"Are you sure?" I asked, still worried about all the things that could go wrong. I'd managed well enough in front of the Council today, but for a person as shy as I was, the idea of meeting my boyfriend's family was nerve-wracking. What if I couldn't control my anxiety around them?

"Devin's parents are very kind, so you need not be nervous," Rayden said.

"After everything that's happened these past few months," Devin said. "I think it's about time life went back to normal. Obviously, that's going to take time, but I figure meeting my family is a good place to start."

"I'm still getting used to having a mother, and a cousin, and living in a new home," I said, struggling to find the right words to voice my thoughts. "Not to mention this whole magic thing. It's a lot all at once. I'm worried I won't make a very good first impression."

Devin reached for my hand, twining his fingers through mine. "Are you not happy here?"

"No, that's not it at all." I actually loved the Wilds. The little of it I'd seen was enough to convince me this was the most breathtakingly gorgeous place ever. Everything felt more alive here, colors seemed more vivid, the air fresher. So there was no internet or TV, but I didn't miss those things, and I quickly realized that magic made up for the lack of technology. A simple spell turned a tub full of cold bath water into the exact temperature one desired.

"I imagine I know a little about how you feel," Devin said. "I never quite got used to the human way of doing things, but when I was with you in Crescent City, I didn't mind. All that mattered was that we were together."

The way he said it took me back to that time. In between the sad memories of losing my dad and then having to leave my home in the middle of the night to keep Zoran from finding me lay some of my happiest. Lying in Devin's arms at night, spending windy days at the beach with him watching the waves as they crashed into the shore, our first kiss.

Suddenly, I wished we weren't expected at my mother's for dinner so it could be just the two of us again like it had been for those few quiet months we'd had together before my life got turned upside-down.

Chapter 6

The aroma of spiced meat greeted Devin, Rayden and me as we arrived at my mother's house later. My stomach grumbled, reminding me that I hadn't eaten since breakfast.

"Dinner is almost ready," my mother announced as Devin shut the door behind us. I watched as she added the last few ingredients to the pot in the fireplace and sliced a loaf of bread, which she put into a basket and placed on the already-set table.

Her house was bigger than Rayden's and more finely appointed. Every time I'd visited her I somehow got the feeling my mother wasn't comfortable with all the finery, as if the fancy area rug or elaborately carved furniture had been someone else's idea. Or maybe it was the thought that she'd shared this place with a man she loathed for so many years that made her seem out of place in her own home. Perhaps once Zoran was truly gone, she could find a place that was more her style and didn't hold so many bad memories.

"Is there some way I can help?" I asked.

"No need." My mother lifted the cast iron pot from the fireplace and brought it over to the table. "Shall we eat?"

Rayden ladled stew into our bowls and then sat down and lifted his cup of pear cider. "Here's to family dinners," he said, an infectious smile on his face. Rayden was truly one of the most cheerful people I'd ever met.

We followed Rayden's lead, lifting our cups into the air before drinking. Ciders of all kinds were another popular beverage in the Wilds and were made from every fruit you could imagine, along with some I'd never heard of in the human world.

Because my mother had prohibited any further discussion about the Council or Zoran, dinner was mostly a quiet affair. I worried that any topic I brought up would steer us all back to those two taboo subjects, so I confined my comments to mundane subjects like how delicious my mother's stew was.

⁓

That night, I had a terrible time trying to fall asleep. With Devin gone and Rayden fast asleep in the room across the hall, the quiet left me with too much time to think, and fear gnawed at my insides. I thought back to when I met Zoran for the first time and saw the steely look in his eyes. Was it even possible to stop someone who was that determined to get what he wanted? It had to be, I told myself, because I was also determined. Devin and I had fought hard for our happiness and I wasn't about to let anyone take it away from me. Despite my resolve it took a lot longer than I wanted to push thoughts of Zoran out of my head and fall asleep.

Thanks to my tossing and turning, I woke up later the next morning than I usually did. As I sat up, I noticed a dress hanging from the drawer pull of the armoire in my bedroom. I must've been in a pretty deep sleep not to have heard anyone come into the room. A small note pinned to the dress piqued my curiosity. I peeled back the blanket and got out of bed so I could read it.

Dearest Lilli,

I picked this dress out for you some time ago, anticipating that eventually you'd have an occasion to wear it. Don't feel compelled to, if it isn't your style, but I thought the color would look lovely on you.

Love Always, Your Mother

The dress was a muted teal with little threads of silver woven throughout, had cap sleeves and fell about mid-calf. The gauzy, flowing fabric was similar to the kind used in the other tunic-style shirts and dresses that people in the Wilds seemed to favor, although the color of the dress was brighter than what I was used to seeing. When it came to clothing, people here stuck mostly to shades of gray and brown. Still, it was a pretty dress, and a gift from my mother—the first I'd ever received.

A knock on the door lifted me out of my thoughts.

"Come in."

Devin entered and shut the door behind himself. "You don't usually sleep in this late."

"What do you think of this dress?" I asked, turning toward him and holding it up so he could get a good look at it.

"It will look beautiful on you." He inched closer and put his hand on my waist. "Though you'd look just as beautiful in a sack."

I frowned. "I can't exactly wear one of those when I meet your family, though."

A wide smile stretched across his face, making his eyes sparkle. "So does that mean you've agreed?"

I nodded. It had been silly of me to be so hesitant the night before. Of course I needed to meet Devin's family. Back in Crescent City, before I'd agreed to come with him to the Wilds, Devin had told me that there was no future for him without me in it. And I felt the same, which meant his family would one day be mine. It was about time I finally met them. I took a few steps back and glanced down at the dress. "My mother got it for me. I like it, but I'm worried it's too bright."

"No, it's perfect. Bright colors are for special occasions."

Devin reached for the dress, his grin still wide, and flung it on my bed. His hand snaked around my waist as he pulled me closer and pressed his lips on mine. My heart pounded. I knew Devin could hear, but I'd long ago stopped caring about that. I twined my fingers through his chestnut hair, kissing him back, and letting my tongue slide in between his lips.

"I miss having you in my arms at night," Devin whispered into my ear as he held me in his arms. As badly as I wanted to be with him again, being in my cousin's house stopped us from going further than a few passionate kisses.

"I do, too."

"Then we should do something about it."

"Something like what?"

Devin hesitated before replying. "Something like getting you to agree to marry me. And while we plan for our wedding, my father and I can look for land to build a home. Our home."

With my heart pounding I lifted my head and gazed into Devin's eyes. "Are you asking me to marry you?"

He looked away. "I don't have a ring yet," he admitted. "But I'll get one, in fact I'll get anything you ask me to if you say yes."

"You know I don't care about a stupid ring."

"Well, I do. Because you deserve the best of everything."

I reached for his hands and pulled him close enough to kiss him again. He kissed me back. I closed my eyes, remembering what it had been like to lay in his arms and feel his skin against mine, wanting it more than anything else. "As long as I have you, that's all that really matters to me."

"Then I want you to meet my family as soon as possible. Tonight even. Because we can't exactly plan our future together until that happens."

"Um . . . sure, I guess," I said, nervous, but at the same time excited about Devin's haste.

"Well, I better go tell my mother. Knowing her, she'll want to have a feast prepared." Devin gave me a kiss on the cheek. "I'll return before dinner to bring you with me," he said, making a quick exit before I had a chance to back out.

After he left, I wandered into the main room in search of breakfast. The house was quiet. I assumed Rayden had left earlier to tend to his shop. I poured myself a cup of tea and sat down at the dining table. A piece of paper lay on it a few inches from where I'd set my cup, and I couldn't help but glance at it. An image of Zoran's face, hand-drawn, but a perfect likeness, stared back at me.

Wanted Dead or Alive

Zoran Raeburn, for the crimes of using dark magic and consorting with demons. Anyone with any information as to his whereabouts

is expected to share it with the Council of Witches immediately.
Failure to do so will result in banishment from the Wilds.

I stared down at the face I'd hoped to never see again. Despite that, I found myself relieved that the Council had moved quickly to get the word out about my father.

I looked over at the fireplace in the corner of the room where elemental magic kept a fire burning around the clock to not only warm the house, but also provide a cooking source. I had yet to master cooking over a fire, but I was hungry, so I found some eggs and a cast iron skillet in the kitchen area. I set the skillet down on a metal grate in the fireplace and cracked some eggs into it, scrambling them with a fork until they were cooked the way I liked.

After finishing my eggs, I got dressed, throwing on a belted tunic top over a pair of pants. Earlier, while eating breakfast, I'd decided that I wanted to go see my mother. So after running a brush through my long, stick-straight dark hair, I closed my eyes and pictured her home.

I walked up to my mother's door and knocked. She ushered me inside.

"What a nice surprise," she said. "I wasn't expecting you."

"No visions of your daughter showing up at your door?" I said, only half-joking.

"You know my visions don't work like that. I see *some* things that will happen in the future, not all." While my mother closed the door behind us, I took a seat. "What brings you here?"

"I wanted to thank you for the dress," I said.

"You liked it? I'm so glad." My mother filled two cups with

tea and brought them over to the table where I sat. "As delighted as I am to see you, I get the feeling you're here for more than that."

"What are Devin's parents like?" I asked, jumping right into the reason for my visit. It felt strange asking her for motherly advice. Back in Crescent City, I would talk to my Aunt Kate about things like this, but I couldn't do that anymore.

"Ah. You're nervous about meeting them." She took a sip of her tea before continuing. "You have no reason to be, though. The Ashworths are kind, despite the prejudices they've had to endure, and I know they will love you."

"Enough that they'll accept me into their family?"

Her eyes narrowed. "What do you mean by that?"

I didn't want to tell her about Devin's almost proposal earlier. "I love Devin and he loves me," I said, hoping she'd understand what I meant.

My mother set her cup down on the table. She stared at me like she had something on her mind but was too afraid to say what it was.

"What is it?" I finally asked.

"I'm not sure if you are truly aware of what being with Devin means."

I frowned. "I thought you liked him."

"I do," she insisted. "Very much. But people will talk. They'll want to know what a beautiful girl like you who comes from two powerful families of witches is doing with someone who is so far beneath her."

"Is that what you think?" I asked, anger stirring. "That Devin is beneath me?"

She shook her head. "There was a time, perhaps, that I might have. But after I fell in love with your father . . . I mean, Mark, I realized that the heart wants what it wants. It doesn't care about money or power, or even what race of beings we are."

"So then why did you bring it up?"

"Because although I may not care that Devin is half shape-shifter, Zoran most definitely will." My mother leaned in closer to me. "So as much as it pains me to say this, I think it's safer if the two of you tread more carefully until the Council tracks Zoran down. He will not approve of the two of you being together, and I worry what he might do."

"Zoran can't *do* anything. Who I choose to be with is up to me, not him or anyone else."

My mother sighed and shook her head. "I wish it were that easy. But you have to understand that life in the Wilds is different than life in the human world. We may have rules, but not many of them. Most witches do as they please, especially your father. And if it pleases him to keep you and Devin apart he'll find a way to make it happen."

A strange mix of fear and anger filled me. I shook my head, willing both those emotions away. "I don't want to talk about Zoran."

"You're right. I don't want to talk about him, either." My mother rested her hand on top of mine and smiled weakly. "So when will you be meeting Devin's family?"

"Tonight."

"So soon?" she said. "Perhaps I can help you get ready. I've always dreamed about braiding my little girl's hair."

And I'd always dreamed of having a mother to do that for

me, but it was too late for that. "I'm not a little girl anymore," I said, not sure how I felt about having my hair braided. I usually wore my hair either pulled back in a ponytail or loose.

"I promise I won't put your hair into pigtails."

I gazed into my mother's eyes, still marveling at how much alike we looked, and smiled. "Well, in that case, yes, you can do my hair."

"Then I will meet you at Rayden's later."

Later that afternoon, I changed into the dress my mother had given me and waited for her to arrive. She brought a small basket with her that held a brush and hair pins, which she used to smooth and style my hair. When she was done, I went to my bedroom and studied my reflection in the mirror that hung on the wall beside my armoire. The front of my hair was pulled away from my face and braided intricately while the rest of my hair fell down over my shoulders.

"Do you like it?" My mother had followed me into my bedroom and stood behind me with her hands on my shoulders.

"I love it." I turned around to hug her. All of a sudden, I thought about Aunt Kate and how terribly I missed her. I pulled away, thinking I was glad my mother wasn't a telepath. I wanted to love her, I did love her, but despite the dress and my fancy hairstyle, we were still in the getting-to-know-you phase of our relationship. It was my aunt, not my mother, who'd been there for me for as long as I could remember.

Thankfully, a knock on the front door pulled me out of my thoughts. "It must be Devin," my mother said.

I practically ran to open the door. "Are you ready to go?" he asked as I let him inside.

"Yes." I wiped my sweaty palms on my dress and turned to grab my cloak. Once I had it on I glanced at my mother. "Thank you," I told her, "for everything."

"Of course," she said, her voice barely above a whisper.

Devin took my hand, and I closed my eyes. A moment later we arrived near the front of what I assumed was his house. "C'mon," he said, tugging on my hand.

The door opened before we reached it. A boy, who looked to be around twelve years old, smiled as he gestured for us to follow him inside.

"You must be Sage," I said after he shut the door behind us.

"Yes, and you're Lilli, right? I know because my brother can't stop talking about you. You look just like he described."

I'd never seen Devin blush—until that moment. His parents walked over. Both gave me a hug and a kiss on my cheek before introducing themselves. Kileena had the same sea-green eyes as her eldest son. Tibor's were blue and his hair a sandy blonde. Where Devin looked like his mother, Sage definitely looked like his father.

"We've waited so long to meet you," Kileena said.

"Never mind about that," Tibor interjected. "She's here now, and that's all that matters."

My nervousness evaporated in seconds. Kileena, Tibor and even little Sage were some of the most welcoming and warm people I'd ever met. Dinner was already on the table—some kind of roasted bird that looked like chicken but tasted a bit different than what I was used to. Either way, it was delicious. So were the roasted vegetables served along with it.

While we ate, I was peppered with questions about life in the human world, which was actually a good thing because it kept me from having to come up with things to say on my own—something I wasn't very good at.

After dinner, I helped clear the dishes from the table, but Kileena refused to let me wash any of them. "You're a guest," she said. "Go sit down with everyone else. This won't take me but a minute or two."

The Ashworths' home was far more modest than both my mother's and Rayden's. There wasn't much room to walk around in between the furniture. Perhaps they didn't earn as much money as my cousin did. Devin had once told me that his parents made a living by selling all sorts of products made from glass. They used their ability to control fire to create their glassware.

I made my way over to the seating area and sat down beside Devin.

"My parents love you," he whispered in my ear.

I took his hand, lacing my fingers through his.

"I hoped you enjoyed dinner," Tibor said.

"Yes. It was delicious. Thank you so much for having me over."

He smiled. "It was our pleasure."

A few minutes later Kileena joined us, bringing along with her a tray with steaming cups of tea and an assortment of small cakes. I helped myself to one savoring the lemony flavor.

When it was time to return home later, I made sure to thank Kileena and Tibor for dinner and tell them how happy I was to have met them and Sage. The three of them seemed embarrassed by the compliments.

"We must do this again soon," Kileena said.

"Next time I'll make dinner and you can come over to my house."

Sage looked up at his dad. "Can we?" he asked. "We haven't been to Rayden's in a long time."

Tibor patted the top of his son's head. "Of course we can."

After Devin's parents embraced me I bent down to kiss little Sage on his cheek. Then Devin and I turned to leave.

"Is it okay if we take a walk before we return to Rayden's?" he asked, after closing the door behind us.

"Sure." Devin took my hand. We walked in silence for a few minutes before I asked, "Is something on your mind?"

"Not really," he said.

"Not really means yes, you do have something on your mind, but you just don't want to tell me what it is."

"Okay. I was sort of wondering . . ." He paused and chewed his lower lip before continuing. "I know you said yes earlier when I asked you about getting married, but are you really sure it's what you want?"

"Why would you think it's not?"

"Because it's different in the human world. People there don't get married until they are much older than we are now."

"I know, and believe me, I've thought about that," I said. "But just because we've promised ourselves to each other doesn't mean that we have to run off and get married right away, does it?"

We stopped walking and Devin turned to look at me, running a hand through my hair before resting it on my cheek. "No, of course not. It can mean whatever you want it to. I just want to be with you. I want you to fall asleep in my arms every night and wake up beside me in the morning."

"That's what I want, too."

Devin let out a breath. "You don't know how relieved I am to hear you say that. After I left you this morning, I began to worry that you'd panic about how quickly things between us were moving."

"I haven't been here very long but I've already come to realize that I can't compare the way things are done in the Wilds to the way things are done in the world I grew up in. And I'm fine with that."

Witches didn't overthink love as much as humans seemed to. They fell in love fast and hard, just like Devin and I had. And like my mother and the man who raised me. Maybe that was strange to some people, but to me it seemed like the most normal thing in the world to do.

Devin gazed into my eyes for a moment before kissing me. I shivered, as the electricity I always felt at his touch ran through me.

"I should take you home," he said after a while. "It's getting late. Rayden and your mother are probably wondering when you'll return."

"Will I see you in the morning?" I asked, missing him already.

He smiled. "Nothing could keep me away."

When I returned home I found Rayden and my mother sitting in front of the fire reading. Their heads turned in my direction as I closed the door behind myself.

"How did everything go?" Rayden asked.

"Fine," I replied, hanging up my cloak. "You were right about Devin's family. They are very nice."

"Come take a seat beside us," my mother said. "Tell us more."

I grabbed a chair from the table and brought it over. "Kileena and Tibor are very friendly; they asked me a lot of questions about where I grew up, but not nearly as many as Sage did. He's such a curious boy."

"The Ashworths are good people," Rayden agreed.

"I was kind of wondering something."

"And that would be?" my mother asked.

"Devin's house is so much smaller than this one. Why is that?"

Rayden and my mother exchanged quick glances at each other. "There are a lot of witches who refuse to step foot into their shop because of what Devin is," my mother finally explained. "Some people say that he and his mother are cursed."

"There are quite a few ignorant fools living here," Rayden added.

"You know what I don't get?" I said, trying to keep my cool. "Why is it that witches hate shape-shifters so much anyway? As far as I can see they pretty much stay to themselves." I hadn't encountered a single one since I'd arrived here. Granted, Devin had explained they were mostly nocturnal creatures, and I didn't spend much time roaming through the woods at night, but I'd still expected to have seen one by now.

"Devin never explained?"

"All he told me was that shape-shifters are more animal than human. He hates them because of what his father did to his mother. Which I understand, but at the same time, it's horrible. He is half shape-shifter, after all. It doesn't seem right, him hating half of who he is."

"The shifter who attacked his mother was obviously very

disturbed," my mother said. "But the part about shifters being more animal than human isn't right. I understand that witches don't have a very high opinion of shape-shifters, but if you ask me, they have more of a right to dislike us than we do them."

"Really? Why?"

"Perhaps Devin doesn't know the true story behind the relationship between witches and shape-shifters. It's a shame how little the younger generation of witches knows of our history," my mother remarked.

"Not all of us are as interested in reading as you are," Rayden quipped.

"Well, perhaps you should be. Then you'd have a better understanding of why things are the way they are," she scolded before turning her attention back to me. "Have you ever heard of familiars?"

I shook my head. "I don't think so."

"Hundreds of years ago, when humans and witches lived together, most humans believed that familiars were a certain kind of spirit that witches communicated with. They appeared as animals, and supposedly helped us do all sorts of evil things to humans," my mother explained. "That belief is actually partly true. Except familiars were never spirits. They were shape-shifters. You see, long ago, shape-shifters were our companions, our closest and truest of friends. Witches who had familiars were highly regarded because witches weren't the ones who chose whether or not to have a familiar."

"It was the opposite, right?" Rayden said. "Familiars chose witches."

"That's right. The idea was that only the best of our kind

earned the type of loyalty a familiar gave. For once a witch gained a familiar, he or she also gained blind trust and loyalty. That's how the term familiar came about," she explained. "But some witches took advantage of this gift, asking their familiars to do evil tasks for them. This went on for some time until they said no more. Their kind was tired of being mistreated and wanted nothing to do with witches ever again."

"That doesn't explain why witches hate shape-shifters so much, it only explains why shape-shifters don't like us."

"It's because of how betrayed witches felt when their familiars left them."

"But that's not fair," I said. "It's their own fault."

"Fair or not, that's the story."

I sat back in my chair, absorbing my mother's words. Fair or not, I hated that Devin was paying the price for the bad blood between witches and shape-shifters, enduring comments he unwittingly overheard because of his sharpened senses. It only made me even more determined than ever to show him how precious he truly was.

Chapter 7

In spite of the story my mother shared, I managed to fall asleep easily that night, but I didn't stay that way for long. I woke up sometime in the middle of the night with my heart racing, drenched in sweat from a nightmare unlike any I'd ever had before.

Devin and I had been walking together, holding hands. We were talking and I'd asked him something, but he didn't answer. That's when I realized I no longer felt his hand holding mine. I turned to look for him; he stood a few steps behind me, but when I reached for him he began to fade away, before disappearing altogether.

My rational mind told me I'd only had the dream because I was afraid of losing him, but I still felt overcome with anxiety. I couldn't get back to sleep. Every time I tried, the image of Devin fading away filled my mind. Tired of trying and failing to fall back asleep, I finally got out of bed.

It was just before dawn and the house was still dark, but enough moonlight streaked in through the skylight that I noticed someone sitting on the couch as I entered the main room. For a moment, I was startled, but then I realized it had to be my cousin.

"What are you doing up so early?" I asked.

"I've been waiting for you."

It wasn't Rayden's voice that answered. In the darkened room, I couldn't see the man's face clearly, but I knew who it was. His voice was one I'd never forget.

"What are you doing here?" I stood, frozen in place, not sure what to do.

"I came to see my daughter. What else would I be doing here?"

The light on the table beside the couch flickered on as Zoran passed his hand under an orb set on a bronze stand. No electricity required, just magic. Zoran appeared to feel right at home stretched out on the couch in my cousin's house. He certainly did not come off as a man on the run. The smug look on his face sent a wave of anger roaring through me.

I closed my eyes and let all the pain and fear I'd been bottling in over the past few weeks fill me. With every heartbeat those emotions spread like poison throughout my body. I harnessed the feelings and cast them outward, imagining myself throwing them like a bucket of boiling water over Zoran.

He stared back at me, not even the least bit fazed. If anything, it was disappointment I saw in his eyes. As I refocused, Zoran reached into his pocket and pulled out a small flask.

"I was afraid you'd try to do that," Zoran said. "That's why I came with protection."

"Protection?" I frowned. "What do you mean?"

"This, my dear, is a potion meant to ward off the effects of abilities like yours. So there's no point in tiring yourself out trying to hurt me because it won't work."

Why hadn't Devin warned me about a potion like that? "What do you want from me?" I asked, feeling both helpless and angrier than ever.

"I should think that's obvious. I'm here because I want to see my daughter."

"I. Am. Not. Your. Daughter."

Zoran looked amused, as if I were a small child throwing a tantrum. "Oh, but you are. And that is not something you or anyone else can change."

"I want you to leave now." I pointed toward the door.

Zoran cocked his head to the side and patted the empty spot next to him. "Why don't you come sit next to your father?"

My mind was a jumbled mess, making it impossible for me to figure out the right thing to do. Zoran wasn't above hurting Rayden, so shouting for my cousin would only put him in danger. Same thing held true for summoning one of the Council's Messengers. Still, I couldn't help but to reach for the amulet around my neck.

"Surely you're at least a little curious about what I came to say."

"No. Actually I'm not."

"Stubborn girl," he muttered. "I still wouldn't bother with the amulet, though. Anyone you summon with that will be dead long before they can call for help." Zoran's voice was like ice. "I'm sure that's not something you want on your conscience."

I released the amulet and dropped my hand to my side, certain he wasn't bluffing. "Just say what you came here to say."

"I'm worried about you," Zoran said, crossing his legs. "And not happy about the company you've been keeping."

I frowned. "Excuse me?"

"Your relationship with that half-breed Devin has gone on long enough. He's not an appropriate match for you. Given that you don't understand the way things work here, I'm willing to give you this one chance—"

"Who are you to talk about appropriate matches?" My blood boiled at his pathetic attempt at fathering. "Not that long ago you had no problem marrying me off to some demon!"

Zoran stiffened. "A regrettable decision, but one you know was made before I knew you were my flesh and blood."

"And that's supposed to make it all right?" I was trying my best to keep my voice down, worried I'd wake Rayden, but keeping my temper in check was proving difficult.

"Andras has been taken care of for what he did to you."

"What is that supposed to mean?"

"I couldn't very well leave him unpunished after the way he touched you."

I pressed the palm of my hand to my forehead, which did nothing to ease the throbbing pain in my head. Zoran stood and tried to reach for me, but I backed away before he could touch me.

"Are you okay, my child?" he asked.

"Don't touch me." I glared at him. "Do you honestly think that coming here and telling me you paid Andras back was going to make things right between us?"

Zoran shook his head. "Your mother did you a grave injustice by raising you in the human world. I don't know how things work over there, but nothing I've done is more than what would have been expected of me or any other witch for that matter.

Your mother betrayed me with another man. In our world betrayal like that has a price, and that price is blood. Ask that half-breed who's been lurking around you what he would do if you chose another over him."

"He wouldn't kill anyone over it."

Zoran laughed. "Don't be so sure, my dear. Surely you've told him about Andras. What was his reaction?"

"That's not the same thing."

"I suppose you are right." Zoran sat back down. "Not that it matters, since that half-breed will soon be out of your life."

"That's not up to you to decide," I said, beyond incensed that he'd shown up at the crack of dawn at my cousin's house to tell me he didn't approve of Devin. What made him think he had the right?

"Yes, it is," he said indignantly. "It's like I told you when Sabin brought you to me in the Void, I've grown tired of not getting what I want. I've lost my patience with the Council and their rules against using dark magic. It's made me more powerful than I've ever been—"

"None of that changes the fact that I love Devin."

Anger flashed across my father's face. "He has no right to your love and he knows that." Zoran stood. He suddenly seemed like a giant with his shoulders thrown back, completely unafraid, a man who would do anything to get what he wanted. "I'm your father, so you will do as I say. I'm giving you fair warning. End your relationship with the half-breed, or I'll be forced to step in and take care of things myself."

Before I could form a response, Zoran disappeared, leaving me alone with my anger and fear. I stood there trying to process what had just happened and figure out exactly what he'd meant when he said he'd be forced to take care of things if I didn't break up with Devin. Zoran was on the run, hiding from the Council. How could he possibly take care of anything under those circumstances?

Trembling, I made my way to the dining table and sat down. I sat there frozen for a while before folding my arms in front of me and resting my head on them in an attempt to sort through the jumbled mess my mind had become. The more I tried to convince myself that Zoran was all talk, the louder the voice in my head shouted that Zoran didn't bluff.

When I felt a hand on my shoulder, I practically leaped out of my chair.

"I'm sorry. I didn't mean to scare you," Rayden said. As my racing heart slowed, he sat down beside me. "Are you okay?"

I shook my head. "No, I'm not. You'll never guess who was just here."

"I don't need to guess. I heard when you get out of bed earlier, and when you didn't return to your room, I came to check on you. That's when I heard you and Zoran talking."

"It's a good thing he didn't see or hear you." Suddenly I felt sick to my stomach.

"I'm fairly certain Zoran was hoping that I would overhear your conversation."

I ran a shaky hand through my hair. "Why do you say that?"

"So I could tell you to heed his warning."

"You mean the one about Devin?"

Rayden nodded.

"Well, I'm not going to. I love Devin, we . . . we want to be together." I couldn't bring myself to mention the plans Devin and I had just made for fear that saying the words out loud would jinx us.

"What you want isn't important right now. You need to take your father's warning seriously."

"You can't mean that. I thought Devin was your best friend. Don't tell me you think Zoran is right about him."

"Of course I don't." Rayden took my hand, and I glanced up at him. "Devin is like a brother to me. And even though you and I haven't known each other long, you are my family. I love the both of you. Nothing would make me happier than to dance at your wedding one day, but Zoran will never allow that to happen."

"So we're just supposed to let Zoran tell us what to do?"

The color drained from Rayden's face. He lowered his gaze and shook his head. "He'll kill Devin."

I searched his face for a sign that he didn't actually mean what he'd just said, but there was none. "I won't let that happen," I said.

"You aren't powerful or wicked enough to do what it takes to stop him, Lilli."

"What are you suggesting?"

"You need to convince Devin that you changed your mind about him, that you don't love him anymore, and—"

I wanted to believe Rayden wasn't serious. This wasn't the middle ages where fathers chose who to marry their daughters to. I was legally an adult. I could be with whoever I wanted to. Or at least I could've until I found out I was a witch and belonged to a world with different rules. Now that Zoran knew I was his daughter I couldn't just turn my back on this life. My father would never let that happen. "No! I can't do that!" I wondered if Rayden had even a clue how much he was asking from me. The thought of telling Devin I didn't love him was like a knife going into my chest.

"I'm afraid Zoran won't leave you with a choice."

I got up from the chair and almost toppled over as I tripped on one of its legs. "I can't believe this," I muttered under my breath.

"It won't be forever. After the Council finds Zoran, he'll be powerless to do anything about you and Devin loving each other, but until then—"

"I . . . I can't talk about this anymore." Before Rayden could say another word, I ran off to my bedroom and locked the door. I tried not to be angry with Rayden for what he'd just suggested I do. How could he not see what an impossible thing he was asking? He was supposed to be trying to find a way to help us, not asking me to do the one thing that would shred my heart into pieces.

I paced back and forth across my bedroom floor, finally calming down enough to think straight. The Council would undoubtedly want to know about Zoran's surprise visit. Perhaps something he said or did would provide them with a clue that would help them find him. But I was still too worked up. Before I summoned a Messenger like Lina had taught me to, I needed to talk to someone who would understand. And the only person I could think of that might be able to was my mother. She knew what it was like to have to give up the person she loved. She'd find a way to spare me that same fate.

I threw on some clothes and despite the early hour, went to her home and banged on the door. She was still in her nightclothes, but didn't ask questions as she ushered me inside.

"You really should ask who's at the door before you open it," I said as she closed the door behind us. Zoran's surprise visit had made me paranoid. What if the next house he planned on showing up to was hers? He said he loved my mother, but she'd also betrayed him. What if he planned on making her pay for that?

My mother smiled. "Your concern is sweet. But I already knew you were coming."

I frowned. "You had a vision?"

My mother nodded.

"What else did you see besides me coming?"

"That was it," my mother replied hesitantly. "Why? Did something happen I should know about?"

"Zoran showed up at Rayden's this morning," I said.

My mother's eyes widened. "What did he want?"

"To tell me that if I don't break up with Devin, he's going to kill him."

"Did he give you any idea of where's he's been or what he's up to?"

I'd expected a different reaction from my mother than that. Something along the lines of disbelief and defiance. "No," I said, irritated. "He said what he came to say and then he left."

"And you just let him get away?" My mother grasped my arms. "Lilli, I know you're not comfortable using your powers, but you have them for a reason."

I pulled my arms free. "My powers don't work against him anymore," I explained. "He said he drank some kind of potion that made him immune to them."

My mother's face blanched. She looked on the verge of fainting. "He's not supposed to have that kind of magic," she said, her words coming out stilted.

"Yeah, well, supposed to or not, he does."

My mother turned and walked away.

"Where are you going?" I called after her as she headed down the hall toward her room.

"To get dressed."

I crossed my arms and just stood there waiting for her. A few minutes later she returned, walked over to me, grabbed me by my wrist rather abruptly and pulled me after her.

"Hey. Where are you taking me?"

"To see the Council. We have to tell them what's going on; they'll know what to do."

My mother began to recite the same incantation I had been taught by Lina. The words were barely out of her mouth when there was a knock at the door. My mother opened it to find a cloaked figure standing outside.

Chapter 8

With her hood obscuring her face it wasn't until Lina pulled it back that I realized it was her. Without bothering to usher her inside first, my mother told Lina about Zoran's visit. As soon as the words were out of my mother's mouth, Lina grasped both our hands and took us directly to the Council's compound. The courtyard was empty. Everything seemed eerily quiet, like we had come upon a deserted building in the middle of nowhere. Except something was different this time. Large shadows moved in circles on the ground in front of me. Curious where they were coming from, I looked up and saw two huge beasts flying overhead.

"What are those things?" I asked.

"The Council's gargoyles," my mother replied.

I looked into the courtyard and noticed the two statues that were there the last time were gone. Griffins was what Devin had called them when I'd asked. Half-lion, half-eagle. That hadn't been a big deal when I'd thought they were just statues.

"But they're made of stone," I said. "How is that possible?"

"They are only made to look as if they were made of stone."

My mother tugged on my hand. "Come, they won't hurt you. Gargoyles are trained to know friend from foe."

I managed to pull my eyes away from the flying beasts and we stepped in to the courtyard. My mother and I just stood there watching while Lina conjured tables and chairs. Before long, the courtyard looked like it had a few days earlier when I'd come with Devin and Rayden. A long table with chairs and then two more chairs across from the table appeared. I stared at Lina, still awestruck by the ability to make objects appear out of nowhere.

"Wait here," Lina said. She disappeared inside the compound while my mother took my hand and led me to one of the chairs.

"I wish I knew how to do that." I imitated Lina's hand movement.

"Oh, I bet you could if you were taught how. But the Council forbids anyone but themselves and their Messengers from conjuring."

"That doesn't seem fair."

"It might not be, but can you imagine if people were free to practice magic with no limitations?"

I thought about that as we sat waiting for the Council. It made sense. Limitless power in the wrong hands was a frightening thought. It seemed to be what Zoran was after, and I shuddered to think of what he'd do if he succeeded in getting it. Although, in the right hands, that kind of power would give the defenseless the protection they needed. I guessed that was why the Council was able to use all sorts of magic the rest of witchkind wasn't. But I wondered if it was smart to put that much faith in the Council. Surely they were just as fallible as anyone else. Look how wrong they'd been about Zoran.

After several anxious minutes, the door to the compound opened, and the Council members streamed into the courtyard and sat down.

Just like before, Syre was the first to speak. "You had a visitor this morning."

It was hard for me to tell whether he was making a statement or asking a question. Something about authority figures always made me nervous. I reminded myself I had nothing to be afraid of. We were on the same side. I swallowed the lump in my throat and nodded.

"Tell us everything."

I took a deep breath. Everything had happened so quickly this morning. First Zoran's visit, then mine to my mother's, and now she and I were facing the Council once more. It was amazing but also frightening to think of how many things could take place in a short period of time.

I began by explaining how I hadn't been able to sleep and had gotten out of bed to go to the kitchen for some water when I noticed someone sitting in the living room.

"So Zoran was just sitting in your home waiting for you to get out of bed?" asked Ina.

"Yes," I replied. They cast sideways glances at each other as I explained that I'd tried to use my ability to debilitate Zoran, but it hadn't worked.

"He's grown more powerful than any of us anticipated," Tressa said, leaning back in her chair.

"Because he's using dark magic," Marus replied, his expression stern. "Which is why we have to stop him as soon as we can. The longer it takes, the more powerful he'll become."

"He is but one man," Ina interjected.

"By now I suspect he's amassed a group of followers," Syre said. "We should not underestimate how much of a threat he is, not just to us, but to the rest of the citizens of the Wilds and perhaps even beyond."

"There's something else I have to tell you," I said. When the attention of the Council was back on me, I continued. "Zoran doesn't approve of my relationship with Devin. He told me that if I don't end things with him, he'll take care of it himself."

"That's a rather simple problem," Sana said, crossing her arms. "Tell Devin you can't be with him."

Syre gave her a reproachful look before turning his attention back to me. "I'm afraid there's not much we can do to help you right now."

My heart sank. I didn't know why I'd expected they could, but hearing them confirm it was still a disappointment.

"Is there anything else?" Marus asked.

"No." I shook my head. "That was it."

"Very well then," Syre said. "Lina, please return Lilli and Naiara home."

She stepped forward, walking toward my mother and me. We both stood and gave Lina our hands. A few moments later, we were back in front of my mother's home. Worry weighed on my mind in a way that I knew meant I wouldn't be good company. What I needed was to go somewhere, alone, so I could release my pent-up emotions. I assumed that by now Devin had probably already shown up at Rayden's to look for me. I prayed my cousin had the sense to give Devin a reasonable excuse for why I wasn't home.

"I . . . I'm sorry," I said, backing away as my mother took a step closer to me. "But right now, I need to be alone."

Before my mother could protest or ask where I was going I closed my eyes and pictured the meadow Devin had taken me to the other day.

Dawn had given way to a bright and sunny morning, but it hardly mattered. My mood was so dark I couldn't think straight. Between Zoran's surprise visit and his threats, and realizing the Council wasn't even close to tracking him down, I was more on edge than I had been in a long time.

I walked over to the same tree Devin and I had sat under the other day and pressed my back against the trunk. Then I covered my face with my hands. Even though I didn't want to cry, hot angry tears rolled down my face as I replayed Rayden's warning in my mind. I was too tired to remain standing. After sitting I lowered my head onto my bent knees, which was why I didn't realize I wasn't alone anymore until I felt a hand on my shoulder.

As I looked up, Devin's handsome face instantly lifted my mood. "How did you know I was here?" I asked.

"I just had a feeling." He sat down beside me. "Should I have stayed away?"

I shook my head. "No. I'm glad you found me."

He put his arm around me and I leaned into him. "Do you want to tell me what's going on?"

Truthfully, I didn't want to, but it was obvious something was bothering me, so there was no point in lying. "Zoran paid me a visit this morning."

"What!?" Devin grimaced. "Are you okay? He didn't try to hurt you again, did he?"

I shook my head. "I'm his daughter, remember?"

"Right," Devin muttered. "What did he want?"

I struggled to think how to answer Devin's question because I didn't want to tell him about Zoran's threats. "He just wanted to see his daughter," I said, trying to keep myself from stuttering.

Devin frowned. "I can't believe he'd be that bold."

"He didn't seem even the least bit worried about the Council." Devin took my hand as I explained the rest of my morning to him. The only part I left out was Zoran's threats. They weren't important, I reasoned, still convinced that no one was going to tell me what to do.

"Don't worry, Lilli. They'll catch him. They have to." Devin put his hand on my chin and tilted my head so I could look into his eyes. "I'm sorry that I haven't been able to shield you from all of this. Sometimes I think you would've been better off if I'd never told you about witches and the Wilds or your mother being alive."

I shook my head. "None of this is your fault. If you hadn't told me, I would've found out some other way." My mother tried so hard to change her visions of the future only to fail in the end. "Everything that has happened to me so far was destined." As the words left my mouth, I couldn't help but wonder what else destiny had in store for me. I wasn't sure I really wanted to know.

Devin dropped his hand from my chin and leaned back. "I still can't believe Zoran visited you. It's so brazen. It's like he's a step ahead of us, and I hate that."

"A step? More like a few hundred miles. He's more powerful than ever, and no one knows where to find him. By the time he shows up again, who knows what he'll be able to do?"

"I refuse to believe that Zoran will win." Devin's eyes flashed angrily. He reached for my hand. "We'll figure something out. Zoran is not meant to win. We are. After everything you've been through, everything *we've* been through, it's our turn for happiness."

Devin believed every word of what he'd just said, and I loved him for it. At the blackest times of my life, he was there guiding me through, promising that things would be better. He was my lighthouse. Nothing and no one would make me give him up. I reached for him and pressed my lips on his. My hands twined through his hair as I deepened the kiss and leaned toward him, pressing my body against his.

I peeled his jacket off and slid my hands under his shirt, running them over his smooth skin.

"Oh, Lilli," he groaned.

"I need you," I murmured into his ear. We hadn't done more than kissing since arriving in the Wilds, mainly because I was living with my cousin and Devin with his parents and brother. But no one would see us out here. The meadow was empty, and even if it wasn't, the branches of the tree sheltered us from view.

"Are you sure?" Devin asked.

"Please don't tell me we're back to that."

When we'd first got together Devin had been so afraid of taking advantage of me that he wouldn't let things between us go too far, but I was certain we'd gotten past that. I guided one of Devin's hands up my shirt, bringing it to rest on my breast. His breath hitched. Then I kissed his neck, slowly letting my tongue graze over his skin. He uttered a sound like a cross between a moan and a growl.

He snatched his hand out from under my shirt, reached for the hem, and pulled it over my head in one lightning-fast motion. Devin leaned into me, pressing me down and onto my back. The grass under me felt soft, like a warm blanket. For a moment, Devin just looked down at me, staring.

"What's wrong?" I asked.

"Nothing." He shook his head. "It's just hard to take my eyes off you. You're so absolutely and utterly magnificent."

Before I could tell him I felt the same way, he kissed me.

Chapter 9

"How in the worlds have I managed to live without that for the past few weeks?" Devin asked as we lay beside each other afterward.

"It felt like a lot longer than that," I said dreamily.

Devin slowly ran his fingers up and down my arm. "Once I build the perfect home for the two of us, we can do whatever we like whenever we want."

I ignored the ache in my heart those words caused. Zoran had been bluffing. He had too many other things to worry about than his daughter's love life. I refused to lose the man I loved or let my father scare me into thinking I would. "I love you, Devin," I whispered, looking up at him.

He smiled and said, "I love you more," before planting a kiss on the top of my head.

I could've lay in that field, wrapped in Devin's arms, forever, but even in the Wilds, where the pace of life was so much slower, that wasn't a realistic notion. I hadn't eaten a thing all day, and if I was gone too long my mother and Rayden would most certainly worry since I hadn't told either of them where I was going.

After another few minutes, Devin sat up and reached for his shirt. "I was thinking it's about time I showed you around the Wilds, and the best place to start is by taking you to the Markets." He pulled his shirt over his head and stood.

"The Markets?"

"It's sort of like what humans refer to as downtown. Anything that is for sale is found at the Markets."

"Are you sure it will be all right?" I asked hesitantly, anticipating that there would be quite a few other witches out and about by this time of the day.

"If you can handle telling the Council about what Zoran did to you, then you can certainly handle a few gossipy witches." Devin offered his hand and helped me up. "We should start the tour at Rayden's shop. He loves a good surprise."

I thought back to my conversation with Rayden earlier that morning. He expected me to heed Zoran's warning. I wondered what he'd think when Devin and I strolled into his shop together like nothing had happened.

After Devin and I finished dressing he took my hand. "Are you ready?"

I nodded and closed my eyes even though I wasn't sure showing up at Rayden's shop together was such a good idea. When I opened them again, we were standing in the middle of what looked like a town center from one of those black and white pictures in a history museum. There were all sorts of shops and stalls arranged in a circular pattern. Though I couldn't see what they all were, by the smell of fresh baked bread I figured at least one of them had to be a bakery. I looked over my shoulder. A few feet away from us stood a fountain surrounded by a garden full of colorful flowers and benches where people sat talking, others eating.

"That's my parents' shop," Devin said, pointing to a small shop with a thatched roof that reminded me of something I'd seen on a postcard of the English countryside. The word *Glassware* was stenciled in cursive on a shingle that hung from a hook beside the door. "And that one is Rayden's."

It looked almost exactly like his parents' shop except *Apothecary* was written on the sign by the door.

I followed Devin. As the two of us entered, Rayden, who stood behind a large wooden work table where he was filling small jars with what looked like dried herbs, looked up.

His eyes widened. "What are the two of you doing here?" he asked, clearly surprised to see us.

"I wanted to see your shop," I said, looking around. The walls were lined with shelves crammed with jars of herbs and all sorts of other things completely unrecognizable to me. Though each jar was labeled, the handwriting was too small for me to make out what each said from where I stood. A sign on the shelf to my left read *Potion Ingredients,* and the sign on the shelf to my right read *Medicinal Supplies.*

I was so awed that I reacted too slowly when a customer entered the shop. By the time I turned my head, it was too late. She had gotten a good enough glimpse of my face to recognize me.

The woman tinkered with a few jars before making her way over to Rayden with several items in her hands. As Rayden calculated her purchases, she kept glancing in my direction.

"That girl looks just like your cousin Naiara," I heard her whisper to Rayden.

"Does she?" he said with a mischievous grin on his face.

It was obvious she wanted Rayden to say more, but he wasn't about to satisfy her curiosity that easily. After filling her satchel with her purchases, the woman walked over to us. "I haven't seen you in ages, Devin," she said. "Where have you been?"

"Traveling," he replied curtly.

"Are you going to introduce me to your friend?" she asked, with a hint of annoyance.

I met Devin's eyes and nodded. He turned his head to face the woman standing in front of us. "Neela, this is Lilli."

"Nice to meet you," I said, extending my hand. She shook it, her eyes transfixed on me.

"You look so much like . . ." Neela stared at me in silence for a moment. "But you can't be."

"Naiara is my mother," I said, answering the question she was too timid to come right out and ask.

"Your what?" She furrowed her brows in confusion. "I didn't think Naiara had any children."

"Well, it's a long story, and now isn't the time for it," Devin said, trying to shut her down.

"That's all well and good, but you'll have to tell it sooner or later. You know how good people are at making up their own stories if you don't give them the right one."

"Let them," Devin said.

With a sneer on her face she turned and walked away.

"What's her deal?" I asked, wondering if she'd been trying to give us a fair warning or if she'd just made a threat.

Rayden chuckled. "There's nothing that witches like more than a good bit of gossip."

I supposed that was a by-product of living in a small community. For some reason witches didn't have many children. One or two was typical, three was a rarity. As a result the population in the Wilds was rather small, just like it had been in Crescent City where I'd grown up, which was how I knew the way small town people liked to talk.

"Maybe we should've just explained," I said. Neela was right. If we didn't supply a story, people would just make one up.

"We'll have plenty of time to share whatever we feel like later. Right now, you and I need to eat." Devin glanced at Rayden. "Would you like to join us?"

"No thanks. I'm not really hungry, and besides, you two don't need me tagging along. Enjoy your time together."

The words "while you still can" seemed to hang in the air. I wanted to tell Rayden he was wrong. That Devin and I had all the time in the world, but of course Devin would then want to know what I was talking about.

I didn't ask where we were going as Devin led me outside and down a raised walkway made out of wide wooden planks. Every few feet we passed the same *Wanted* leaflet with my father's image that I'd found on the table at home a few days ago. They were posted everywhere. We also passed a store that sold sweets and one that sold housewares before stopping in front of a place with a sign that read *Tabitha's Tavern*.

Devin held the door open for me. Inside, a staircase was located a few feet from the entrance, which I assumed led to rooms upstairs. Off to the right was a large dining area with tables in an assortment of sizes. No hostess waited at the front to seat anyone, so I followed Devin as he led me to an empty table.

"How does this work?" I asked after we sat down. "Does someone come by with menus?"

"No menus. Tabitha or one of her family members will come to our table and let us know which meals are being served today. It changes every day."

My stomach rumbled. The smell of spiced meat had hit me the minute I'd walked through the door. Even if I wasn't hungry, the aroma inside the restaurant was enough to make my mouth water. Thankfully, a woman with reddish-brown hair who looked to be about my age walked over to our table only a few minutes later. She greeted Devin before turning her attention to me.

"I'm Tabitha." She held her hand out for me to shake. After I did, she continued. "No use pretending I don't know who you are. You have to be Naiara's relation."

"I'm her daughter," I said. "My name is Lilli."

"Pleased to meet you." She had such a warm smile that I found myself returning it despite how uneasy the stares I couldn't help but notice were making me.

"So what do you two think I should do when everyone in here starts asking me questions about you?" Tabitha asked, looking down at me with knowing eyes. "Tell them to mind their business, or let them know who you are?"

Devin spoke first. "Tell them to mind their own business—"

"It's okay, Devin." I put my hand over his. "People will find out eventually."

"Yes, they will," Tabitha agreed. Her eyes darted back and forth between me and Devin. "Well, now that that's out of the way, how about I tell you what's being served today?"

"I smell hotpot, don't I?" Devin said. "If I'm right, I'd love a bowl of that."

"You have a good nose."

"I'd like the same," I chimed in, figuring if Devin liked it so much, I probably would, too.

Tabitha smiled and gave a nod before walking away. Not a minute later, two bowls, spoons and napkins appeared on the table. Startled, I jerked back in my chair.

Devin laughed, enjoying the bewildered expression on my face. "I should've warned you about that."

"You think?"

A moment later the bowls in front of us filled with what looked like some sort of meat stew. I reined in my surprise this time and reached for my spoon. Hotpot turned out to be some sort of spiced meat stew with potatoes and onions, and it was mouthwateringly delicious. The meat fell off the bones, and the potatoes were cooked perfectly, neither too mushy nor too firm.

"This is so good."

Devin smiled. "Don't tell Tabitha, or she'll get a bigger head than she already has now."

"Big head? She seemed really nice to me."

"Oh, she is," he replied. "But she likes to brag that her tavern serves the best food in the Wilds."

"Is she wrong?"

"I wouldn't have brought you here if she was."

Despite how delicious my stew tasted, it was hard to truly enjoy it with so many curious eyes glancing at me. I knew Devin had to be feeling the same way. "How long do you think it will take before people stop staring at me like I'm a unicorn?"

"If you were a unicorn, people wouldn't be staring," Devin said. "They're not nearly as uncommon as human stories make them out to be."

"Are you telling me that unicorns really do exist?"

"Yes. As do fairies and elves. You've already seen the gargoyles outside the Council's compound. There's also mermaids and dragons. But dragons aren't very common. I've only ever seen one in my entire life."

"You're kidding me, right?"

"I've told you before that all manner of magical creatures live not just here in the Wilds but in other magical worlds as well. Did you think I was joking?"

Back when he'd explained all that to me, I'd actually thought he was crazy. It took my seeing him teleport away to believe he hadn't been lying. Still, it was hard to wrap my mind around it all sometimes.

"With so many interesting beings roaming around, you'd think people wouldn't be so interested in me. I'm just a witch like everyone else here."

"It's like Rayden said, witches are the worst gossips," Devin explained. "And you've got quite the story. People are probably wondering where you've been for all these years, and why Naiara and Zoran's daughter has only now surfaced. They're also most likely wondering what you're doing holding hands with someone like me."

"How would they know Zoran is my father?"

"Well, because if you weren't, there's little chance you'd still be alive. Everyone here knows Zoran well enough to expect that he wouldn't let you live if you were another man's child. The humiliation alone would be too much for him to bear."

"If everyone knows Zoran so well, shouldn't the Council already have been aware of how ruthless he is? Why didn't they do anything about it?"

"The Council doesn't involve themselves in personal affairs. That is not their purpose."

That seemed crazy to me, but it explained their nonchalant attitude earlier when I'd told them about Zoran's threats against Devin. Perhaps their expectation was for the two of them to duke it out themselves, although that didn't seem fair, given that Devin was at a clear disadvantage. I reminded myself once more that I needed to stop applying the rules of the human world to the magical one.

"Can you hear what people are whispering?" I asked.

"They're assuming you were kidnapped. And that Zoran has turned to dark magic to avenge whoever is responsible."

"Kidnapped?" Somehow, the idea seemed ridiculous to me. Not that the truth was any more believable.

"Like Neela said earlier, when people don't know the full story, they have a tendency to fill in the blanks with their own ideas."

"Well, what am I supposed to do? Go stand outside and announce to everyone passing by that my mother hid me from Zoran because she had a vision that one day he'd kill me?"

"No, of course not. Eventually, people will stop staring. You'll see."

"I really hope so."

After we finished our meal Devin left a few coins on the table. Being that this was my first true outing, I had no idea about the way money worked here and made a mental note to ask about it later. We stepped back outside and Devin took my hand, leading me in the opposite direction from Rayden's shop.

"Where are we going?"

"There's something I've been meaning to buy for you for quite some time," he said.

I was too put off by all the stares from people we passed by to ask what. We stopped in front of a shop with the same simple sign Rayden had on his shop's door, except this one read *Weapons*.

"Why are we going in here?"

"Because you need to be prepared to defend yourself."

Devin led me over to a display case filled with daggers of all sizes. The owner of the shop got up from his stool. "Good day, Devin. Are you looking for anything in particular?"

"Just a basic dagger and sheath for my lady here."

The shop owner eyed us suspiciously. Like Neela, it was obvious he had questions, but instead of asking them, he pulled out a few daggers for us to examine. Every weapon in the shop looked more like a museum piece than an actual weapon someone would use. But I knew better than that. Devin kept a dagger tucked under his pants leg. It was the weapon he'd used to kill the tracker demon Zoran sent searching for me after he'd learned of my existence.

A lot of people in Crescent City carried weapons—mostly guns—for self-defense and hunting. I supposed a dagger wasn't that different. But my dad never owned any. He didn't like guns, so the idea of carrying a weapon around didn't sit well with me.

I watched Devin while he inspected the first dagger in his

hand. "I think this one is too heavy," he said and handed it to me.

"I just don't see myself ever using a dagger," I whispered as Devin pressed the cool metal handle into my hand. I hoped the shop owner wouldn't take my reluctance as an insult.

"I'd feel much better knowing you had one with you," Devin said. "Everyone here does. It doesn't mean you'll use it, but just in case, it's better to be prepared."

Devin had told me once that one of the only ways to kill demons was to stab them in their chest where their heart would be if they had one. I doubted I'd ever have the guts to do something like that. Knowing myself, I'd probably just freeze in fear.

Just as I was about to set the dagger back down on the counter, I heard my name being called. I was quite sure I didn't know anyone in the Wilds outside of Devin and my family, so I couldn't even imagine who it was. Hesitantly, I turned my head to see.

Kees. Though it had been a few weeks and the Void was a rather dark place, I recognized him right away. A smile spread across his face as he walked toward me. "It's really you," he said. "I've been so worried. Thank the worlds you're all right."

He threw his arms around me before I could respond. Anger flashed in Devin's eyes. I loosened myself from Kees's grasp.

"How do you know Lilli?" Devin asked, his jaw clenched.

I'd told the Council about Kees's role in summoning Andras, but Devin must've been so upset by then he hadn't paid attention to that detail.

"Kees . . . Kees was . . . he told me where Zoran was keeping me," I said, searching for the right words to defuse Devin's growing anger. "If it wasn't for him, you and my mother would never have found me."

"I remember now," Devin said, his eyes still blazing. "And it's the only reason I don't have my hands around his neck." He glared at Kees. "But that doesn't mean I've forgiven you."

"It's not *your* forgiveness I care about," Kees said disdainfully.

While Devin and Kees were arguing, a few people had entered the store. Sensing the tension, their eyes filled with curiosity.

"Can you two stop?" I whispered. "People are looking."

"I'm sorry, Lilli." Kees took a step backward and bowed slightly. "I only wanted to say hello."

"Stay away from her," Devin warned, snaking his hand around my waist.

The words were barely out of his mouth when I felt the strange pulling sensation that came with teleporting.

I struggled to stay on my feet as we arrived in front of my cousin's door. Devin reached out to steady me.

"Next time could you warn me before you do that?"

"I'm sorry. I wasn't thinking," Devin mumbled.

"Why are you so upset anyway?"

"How else do you expect me to react when a man walks up to you and embraces you right in front of me? And not just any man, but one who helped Zoran hold you prisoner and summon a demon." Devin's voice shook with anger.

"Kees only did those things because he was afraid of what Zoran would do to him," I explained.

"Maybe you can forgive him, but I can't," he said, his hands balled into fists. "And besides, he saw us holding hands, which means he knows you're mine. If he touches you again, I swear he'll regret it."

So Devin was jealous. I would've smiled if he wasn't so upset. "I think Kees was just so relieved I was still alive that he didn't notice you standing beside me." I reached for Devin's hand.

He narrowed his eyes. "It was more than that. I saw it in the way he looked at you."

I would've told Devin he had nothing to worry about, but he was so angry I doubted anything I said would have made much of a difference. I tugged on his hand instead. "C'mon. Let's just go inside."

"Not right now," he said, his voice still tense. "There's something I have to do."

He kissed me quickly and disappeared before giving me a chance to ask him what it was.

Chapter 10

Without Devin or my cousin around, the house was eerily quiet. I picked up the copy of *A History of the Wilds* Rayden had given me and absentmindedly began to re-read it from page one.

The Wilds had existed for as long as every other world had. Since the beginning of time, witches, humans, and other magical creatures roamed freely amongst each other. As the human population grew, witches and humans began to encounter each other more and more frequently. At first those encounters were friendly, but over time that changed. When the witch trials began in Europe and the New World, it was decided that witches would take refuge in the Wilds, where no human could ever go. Too many innocent people had lost their lives. Ironically, most of them were humans who had been wrongly convicted of witchcraft.

There were paths into the Wilds all over the human world hidden deep in forests or at the bottom of lakes, but even if a human ventured near one, magic turned them back around. That same magic meant many types of human technology just didn't work in the Wilds. Not that it mattered; it seemed like there was very little one couldn't do with magic.

I was deep into my reading when I heard a knock at the door. For a moment, I froze, afraid that Zoran had returned; but if it was him, I realized, he wouldn't have bothered with knocking.

"Who is it?" I asked from behind the closed door.

"It's Kees."

I reached for the knob, but stopped before turning it. Devin would not be happy. "I don't think you being here is a good idea."

"Please, Lilli. I just want to talk to you. I mean no harm. I swear."

Hesitantly, I opened the door to let him in.

"How did you know where to find me?"

"Teleporting leaves a magical trace. I followed yours."

"What do you want from me?" I asked, not appreciating that I'd been followed.

"I don't *want* anything from you. I just want to tell you how deeply sorry I still am for not standing up to Zoran. I should've made him—"

"No one makes Zoran do anything," I said. "He would've killed you if you'd tried."

"I haven't been able to stop thinking about you since I helped Sabin and Zoran summon that . . . that demon. I even tried teleporting back to where Zoran was keeping you in the Void to see if you were okay. But you were gone, and it looked like there had been some kind of earthquake. I thought the worst, that Zoran had used his powers to bury you under a pile of rubble. It wasn't until the Council summoned me that I learned you were alive. You can't imagine how relieved I felt."

"Glad to know my survival eased your conscience," I replied, dryly. Kees looked at me like I'd just slapped his face. I felt ashamed as I remembered the way Kees had tried to stand up for me, and the way Zoran had punished him for doing so. "Sorry. I didn't mean it to come out like that."

"You have no reason to be sorry." Kees bowed his head. "You were right when you called me a coward."

I put my hand on his arm and Kees looked up meeting my gaze. "Zoran can be intimidating, but you stood up to him anyway, or at least you tried to. I was wrong to call you a coward. If it wasn't for you, I'd probably be dead right now."

"You give me too much credit," Kees said softly. That was something I remembered about him, his mild demeanor, which stood in such stark contrast to Zoran's and Sabin's.

"If you don't mind me asking, besides the part about me not being dead, what else did the Council tell you?"

"That you're Zoran's daughter."

"So you know."

Kees nodded. "I take it you're not happy about that."

"Why would I be? He's a monster."

"You're nothing like him," Kees said. He stared into my eyes. "Lilli, there's something I'd like to ask of you."

"And what would that be?"

"Your friendship."

Unsure how to reply, I looked away without saying a word. I didn't have many friends, and Kees really did seem like a nice person, not that I knew him well. But Devin wouldn't like it.

"Hear me out," Kees began. "I don't want to cause trouble between you and Devin. But if we were to ever bump into each other somewhere, I'd like it if you'd say hello, and maybe stop and talk to me for a bit. That's all I'm asking for."

"Well, if that's all, then I suppose it's okay."

Before Kees could offer a reply, the door opened. Rayden had returned home. He frowned at Kees after closing the door behind himself. "What are you doing here?"

"He was actually just about to leave," I said, preferring to wait until Kees left to explain everything to my cousin.

"Yes, you're right, I was. It was nice seeing you again, Lilli." He glanced at Rayden. "And you, too Rayden. It's been a long time."

My cousin stared at Kees as he walked out. It wasn't until he was sure Kees was gone that Rayden turned his gaze back to me. "So are you going to tell me why he was here?"

I sighed and walked over to the table, taking a seat before launching into a description of our chance encounter at the weapons shop earlier and how Kees had followed me, hoping for an opportunity to apologize.

"I think you're being too easy on him, Lilli. If Kees was really interested in your well-being, he could've asked your mother or even me if we knew what happened to you."

"Maybe he was too ashamed to face either of you. He probably figured I told you guys he'd been helping Zoran."

"That doesn't make what he did all right."

"I know, I know. But he asked for my forgiveness and I gave it to him. End of story."

"You've a very kind heart, Lilli."

"Do you know Kees well?" I asked.

"Not really, but he's always seemed nice enough. Still, I'm not sure how Devin will feel about the two of you being friends—" Rayden paused mid-sentence, as if something suddenly occurred to him. He sat down in the chair closest to me before continuing. "Which gives me the perfect idea."

I frowned. "What are you talking about?"

He looked up at me. "We never did get to finish our conversation from earlier this morning. The one where I told you that the only way to keep Devin alive was to break things off with him."

Rayden's words felt like a slice through my heart. "Are you kidding me? We're back on that?"

"I know you don't want to be. Neither do I, believe me. But I cannot stand by and do nothing knowing what will happen if you don't heed my warnings. My best friend will lose his life, and you'll spend the rest of yours blaming yourself. That's not a fate I want for either of you."

I crossed my arms. "There has to be another way."

"Not until the threat from Zoran is eliminated."

Other than the "Wanted" signs sent out to peoples' homes and posted in the town center, nothing the Council had done so far had given me much faith in them. Still, I couldn't bring myself to believe they wouldn't be able to stop Zoran before he did anything to Devin.

"After everything Devin and I have been through together, how am I supposed to just turn around and tell him I've changed my mind and don't want to be with him anymore? He won't believe it. He knows how much I love him."

"Convince him you've fallen for someone else. Kees is handsome enough with his blond hair and blue eyes, and he comes from a good family. A powerful family. He's the kind of witch you're expected to be with."

"That's your brilliant idea?" I asked, trying to control my temper. "Devin has spent his entire life feeling inferior because of who his father is and because he doesn't come from the 'right' family, and now you expect me to tell him the reason I can't be with him anymore is because I found someone better?"

Rayden grasped my hands. "What I expect is for you to be brave and selfless enough to save his life, the same way your mother was brave and selfless enough to try to save you and the human she fell in love with all those years ago. I know what I'm asking isn't easy, but I also know this is Zoran we're talking about, which means there is no other choice. He was a pompous bully even before he found out about you, but with all the dark magic he's been using, he's far worse than ever."

I wanted to be angry with my cousin, and tell him to mind his business, but when I saw the fear in his eyes, I knew it hurt him almost as badly to say those words as it did to hear them. Zoran was ruthless. No one knew that better than I did. And until he was caught, there was no telling what he'd do.

"Can't I just tell Devin what Zoran said? We could pretend to be broken up until the Council finds him."

"If Zoran even suspects that you or Devin are trying to deceive him, then Devin will be the one to pay." Rayden shook his head. "I'm sorry, but the only choice you have is to make Devin truly believe you don't love him anymore."

His words were like a slap. I felt light-headed. "I . . . I just can't. You don't know what you're asking." I bit my lower lip to keep myself from crying.

Rayden sighed. "Let's not think of this anymore tonight. Tomorrow is another day. Maybe, after what you told the

Council this morning, they'll figure out a way to find Zoran before the sun comes up."

"Do you think that's a possibility?"

"Sometimes all we have is hope," he said. "It may not be much, but it's better than nothing."

I wasn't sure I even had that. The idea of breaking Devin's heart, of being apart from him, even if it was only temporary, made me sick to my stomach. This wasn't supposed to be happening. After going through what I had with Zoran in the Void, Devin and I were supposed to have our happily ever after.

"I'm not feeling very well. I need to go lie down," I said, standing and backing away from my cousin before heading to my bedroom.

I stayed there for the rest of the night. When Devin came over later, I heard Rayden explain that he'd given me something to soothe my nerves because I wasn't feeling well, so I'd be asleep until the morning.

That turned out to be as far from the truth as one could get. All night I lay in bed with my eyes wide open. A few times I fought the temptation to knock on my cousin's door and ask him if he really could compound a calming potion for me, but I knew when I woke up, things would be the same. Zoran would still be free and growing more and more powerful, determined to follow through on whatever plans he had for the Council—and for Devin.

Early the next morning, Devin showed up just after Rayden left for the day. Despite my cousin's warnings, I couldn't keep myself from opening the door and practically falling into Devin's arms. As I stood there with him holding me, I realized there was just no way I had the strength to do what Rayden told me needed to be done.

"Are you feeling better this morning?" Devin asked.

"Yes," I said, nodding as I fought to hide my fatigue. "I think I just needed a good night's sleep."

"Are you sure that's all?" he asked, trying to get me to look into his eyes. "Because if it's not, you know you can tell me."

I managed a smile. "Of course I do."

"Good." Devin kissed my forehead. "Why don't you get dressed? We can continue your tour of the Wilds after you've had a good breakfast. I've got so much more to show you."

"Is it okay if we skip the tour for today?" Being seen together was too risky. For all I knew Zoran had people spying for him. "I want it to be just us."

"Okay. We can hang out here then if you like." He brushed my hair back with his hand. "Why don't I make you something to eat while you get dressed?"

"That sounds perfect."

While I put my clothes on, Devin made eggs and brewed a pot of tea. Though it wasn't cold, the warm drink managed to drive away the chill I felt inside. While I ate, I told myself for the one hundredth time that I was worrying for nothing. Devin was here, sitting beside me. Everything would be fine.

After washing the breakfast dishes together, we sat beside each other on the couch. Devin handed me a book titled *Spellcasting.*

"You read," he said, "and I'll answer any questions you might have."

I got comfortable, resting my head on Devin's lap. I read a few pages and then stopped when a question came in my head.

"How hard are these spells to do?" I asked, pointing to the last half of the book. The first half was filled with basic spells, the second with more advanced ones. I'd managed a few of the basic ones on my own, like the one used to turn a bathtub full of cold water warm.

"Being only half-witch and all, I'm not particularly good at spell casting, so I couldn't really tell you," Devin said. "Your mother is the one you should be asking. She's quite talented."

"What about Rayden? How good is he?"

"At one point he was quite good, but ever since his parents died, he hasn't been the same. He's lost much of his interest in learning and reading. It's like when they died, a part of him did, too."

"What happened to them?" I knew Rayden's parents were dead, but I'd never asked how.

"Healers have always been a favorite target of demons. Kill the ones who can cure the sick and injured, and you've just rid yourself of a major obstacle."

"Rayden must've been devastated."

"He was," Devin said. "For a while after they died, he kept making me promise I wouldn't do anything stupid, said he couldn't stand losing another person he loved."

It made sense now, Rayden's reaction to Zoran's threat. My heart dropped.

"I know how he feels. I couldn't stand it, either."

Devin lifted my head from his lap, and I sat up. He wrapped one of his hands around the nape of my neck and looked at me intently. "Then I'm going to tell you the same thing I told your cousin. You won't lose me. Ever."

I wanted to tell him there was no way he could promise that, but then he'd want to know why I was making such a claim, and I didn't want to talk about Zoran. Instead, I buried my head in his chest. His arms circled me.

We were so wrapped up in each other that neither of us heard Rayden come in until he shut the door behind himself with a loud thud. I pulled away from Devin.

Without a word, my cousin hung up his cloak and then went to prepare himself a cup of tea. Devin and I both felt the tension in the air.

"Is something wrong, Ray?" Devin asked.

He shook his head. "No. Nothing," he said while gazing at me with unmistakable disappointment in his eyes.

"You're home early," I said.

"I was hungry."

"Um, you know what. I just realized that my father needed help with something today," Devin said, getting up from the couch. "I promised I'd meet him around lunchtime."

Devin wasn't fooling me. He was leaving because he figured Rayden had something on his mind that he wanted to discuss privately. Not wanting our time together to be over so quickly, I almost pleaded with Devin to stay, but instead I walked him to the door. "Will I see you later?"

"Tomorrow, actually. What my father and I have to do will take the rest of the afternoon."

He kissed me before crossing the room. After Devin left, I turned to face Rayden, bracing myself for the lecture he was sure to give me. He didn't say a word to me though. After a few tense minutes I realized his silence was even worse. I couldn't stand being in the same room with his accusing eyes on me, so I headed down the hall to my room, where I remained for most of the rest of the day.

Chapter 11

I was in the middle of cleaning up the kitchen the next morning when someone knocked on the door. I opened it, expecting Devin. Instead, it was his mother.

"Is Devin all right?" I asked as Kileena stepped inside.

"He is, for now," she said in a shaky voice. "But that can change in an instant. You do realize that, don't you?"

"What are you talking about?" I asked, warily, wondering what she knew and how she'd found it out.

Kileena crossed the room and sat down. I followed her. "I know Devin has told you the story of his parentage, but there is a part of it he doesn't know," she began. "You see, my attack in the woods the night Devin was conceived wasn't random. I was set up by someone. A friend. At least, that's what I thought we were, until he confessed he had feelings for me—feelings I didn't share. This man . . . he went wild with anger when I told him, vowing to destroy my life the way I'd destroyed his. Of course, I didn't think he really meant it, until that night in the woods."

"I'm so sorry about what happened to you," I said, shocked by her confession. If it hadn't been for Zoran, I would've had a hard time imagining anyone could be that cruel.

"His name was August," Kileena continued. "And if I've ever met anyone who reminded me of him, it's your father, Zoran."

"He's my father by blood only. I'm nothing like him," I said, suddenly afraid of where this was going. When I'd been a guest at her house she seemed friendly and welcoming. Had she changed her mind about me?

"I know that. My son wouldn't have fallen in love with you otherwise." She took one of my hands in hers. "But that doesn't change the fact that by being with you, Devin's life is in danger. And I love him too much to risk losing him."

"Why do you think being with me puts Devin in danger?" I asked, again afraid of her answer.

Kileena looked away. "I don't want you to be angry with him, but Rayden paid me a visit early this morning. He wanted to warn me about what he overheard Zoran saying to you the other day."

A wave of anger rolled through me. What right did Rayden have to get in the middle like that?

As if she read my mind, Kileena continued, "Keep in mind that Devin and Rayden grew up together. They were the most unlikely of friends, yet that's exactly what they are—friends. Which is why Rayden thought I had a right to know that my son's life is in danger."

My heart clenched. "So what are you saying?"

"I'm saying I want you to save my son's life, even if it means breaking his heart and yours to do it."

I stood up and turned my back to Kileena. "I already told Rayden I'd break things off with Devin. He didn't need to go running to you and get you worried for nothing." I was ashamed by the anger in my voice, but I couldn't help myself.

Kileena stood and put her hand on my shoulder, but I couldn't bear to turn and look at her. "Thank you," she whispered before walking out the door, leaving me alone, drowning in my grief.

How had everything gone so terribly wrong? I'd thought nothing could be worse than learning Zoran was my father. I choked back the tears I felt welling in my eyes. The walls felt like they were closing in on me. There had to be something I could do. But what?

I sat there for a while, trying to think, even though my heart hurt like someone had stuck a knife in it. After a while, a plan began to form.

Before Devin and I left Crescent City, we'd visited my Aunt Kate, who lived an hour away in Eureka, to tell her we were leaving California. We'd told her that we had been accepted to a university on the East Coast. It had been a good cover story. She was so happy I was moving on with my life instead of moping over my dad's death that she hadn't really asked too many questions. If I showed up at my aunt's door and told her things between me and Devin hadn't worked out, and that I didn't like being so far from home, she'd try and talk me into going back to school. But if I promised to enroll in Humboldt State, the university near her home, I was certain that would appease her.

Eventually, Devin would find me. He wouldn't stop searching for me until he did, but maybe by then the Council would have captured Zoran, and I could return to the Wilds with Devin again. It would be easy enough to explain to Kate that I'd changed my mind about Devin and decided to get back together with him in the end. She'd probably just shake her head and make a comment about young love, but she wouldn't try to stop me. Kate had always really liked Devin.

As long as our separation was temporary, I could handle being away from him. Especially if I had my aunt to comfort me. And this way, I wouldn't have to look into Devin's eyes and tell him that I didn't want to be with him, or even worse, that I had feelings for someone else, as Rayden had suggested.

My aunt would have a lot of questions if I showed up in the clothes I had on, since the fashion in the Wilds was quite different, so before I lost my nerve, I ran into my room and changed into the clothes I'd worn when I left Crescent City. Even though I had no use for jeans and a T-shirt in the Wilds, I'd kept those old clothes as a memento of a life I hadn't planned on returning to.

I stuffed a small satchel with a few of my belongings and slung it over my shoulder. With closed eyes, I concentrated, picturing the inside of Kate's garage. Maybe it was my nerves getting to me, or maybe it was because the farther you teleported the more difficult it was, but when I opened my eyes again, my heart was booming in my chest and my head felt like it was stuck inside a washing machine.

It took me a moment to get my bearings. After I did, I opened the side door to the garage and walked up to the front of my aunt's house. I took a deep breath, reminding myself of why I was doing this, before finally lifting my hand to press the doorbell. Footsteps pattered toward me. Kate opened the door, but left the screen closed as she peered outside. Something about her expression seemed not quite right.

"How can I help you?" she asked.

"You're funny, Kate," I said, reaching for the handle on the screen door. It was locked. I peered at her, trying to figure out why she was acting so strange.

"Do I know you from somewhere?" she asked, warily.

"Of course you do. I'm your niece, Lilli. Your one and *only* niece."

"I don't know what kind of game you're playing, Miss, but I don't have any nieces," she said, sharply. "And you don't look a thing like my brother, so don't try and convince me you're his long-lost daughter." Kate actually sounded angry. In my entire life, she'd never been angry with me. The fact that she was now left me speechless. Before I could say another word Kate slammed the door in my face. "Leave now, or I'll call the police," she shouted through the closed door.

I lifted my hand to ring her doorbell again, but quickly changed my mind. Something had happened to my aunt, and I intended to find out not only what, but how to fix it. Still, I couldn't help but think that once I walked away, I'd never see my aunt again, and despite the awful circumstances, I had actually been excited at the prospect of spending time with her again.

More than once I had to stop myself from ringing the bell or knocking on the door. If I did, and she made good on her promise to call the police, what would I tell them? I was so stunned by Kate's reaction to me that my head hurt, which made it impossible to think straight. Finally, I managed to peel myself away from her front stoop. I started wandering through the streets near my aunt's home. When I'd decided to run away and return to the human world, I hadn't thought of a plan B. I didn't think I'd need one, so I wasn't sure what to do next.

After walking for a few blocks, my mind began to clear. My mother was a powerful witch. If anyone could fix Kate, I decided, it was her.

I found a secluded area where no one could see me before teleporting back to the Wilds. Once there, I ran up to my mother's house and pounded on her door.

Rayden was inside with her. Alarmed at my expression, my mother said, "What's Zoran done now?"

I shook my head. "Nothing."

"Well, if it's not Zoran, then what's got you so worked up?" Rayden asked.

"My Aunt Kate," I said, biting the inside of my cheek to keep myself from crying. "Something's happened to her. She doesn't remember me."

"Wait. What? How do you know that?"

I sat down and explained. When I was done I looked up at my mother and Rayden. "You can fix her, though, right?"

My mother shook her head. "I'm sorry, Lilli. It doesn't work like that."

"What do you mean?"

"It sounds like someone has erased Kate's memories of you, and the kind of magic it would take to return them isn't something I know how to do, and even if I did, there could be unintended consequences."

"Like what?" I asked.

"It could confuse her beyond the point of repair."

"What do you mean by that?"

"She's already had her memories erased once before, after Sabin tried to get her to tell him where you were. There is only so much manipulation the human brain can handle. Returning memories is a lot more complicated than taking them. It can't be done, Lilli. Not when her mind has been tampered with as much as it already has."

I stared at my mother, trying to process her words, then at Rayden. "Who would do this?" I didn't bother to wipe away the tears that had begun to roll down my cheeks.

"Zoran," my mother muttered. "He's the only one who would have a reason to. He probably wanted to cut all of your ties to the man who raised you."

"But he's . . ." I was so overwhelmed that I couldn't finish my sentence. Zoran was in hiding, but the Council hadn't started looking for him until just a few days ago. He would have had plenty of time to go wherever he wanted and do anything he felt like. Including erasing my aunt's memories.

My mind reeled as everything began to sink in. My aunt Kate, who'd been like a mother to me when, for so many years, I'd thought my real one was dead, didn't even know who I was anymore. How was that even possible?

"There has to be something I can do. Maybe I can use my ability. I can make her *feel* that she loves me. Then she'll remember who I am. I can make all those memories come back."

"It won't work, Lilli," my mother said. Rayden nodded his head in agreement. "I'm sorry. You might be able to temporarily make her feel love, but she still won't know who you are, or even why she's feeling that way, and the minute you leave, those feelings will go away. It'll just confuse her, and if the Council finds out you used your magic on a human like that—"

"I don't really care what they think." No matter what my mother said, I refused to just give up.

"Were you really going to leave the Wilds for good without telling either of us?" my mother asked, sounding hurt at the possibility I'd even considered it.

"It seemed like my best option," I said. "And I wasn't going to leave for good. Just until the Council arrested Zoran."

"Use your head, Lilli," Rayden said, impatiently. "You are a powerful witch who is still learning to master her abilities. Did you really think living amongst humans was a good idea?"

"It's better than convincing Devin that I've fallen in love with someone else."

"I'm sorry, Lilli. This can't be easy on you. I know how much you love him," my mother said. She got up from the table.

I swallowed the lump in my throat. "How did you do it?" I asked. "How were you able to walk away from Dad?"

My mother filled a cup with hot water and tea leaves. She returned to the table and handed me the cup. "Believe it or not, it was because of you."

"Me?" I frowned. "What do you mean?"

"When I fell in love with your father I thought nothing could be more powerful than the feelings I had for him," she said. "Until you came along. I still loved your father as deeply and passionately as ever, but I loved you more. There was not a single thing I wouldn't do, not a sacrifice I wouldn't make, to keep you safe.

"I know telling Devin you've fallen in love with someone else won't be easy, but if it means him staying alive, then I know you'll do what's right," Rayden said.

For the first time, the reality of my situation sunk in. Of course I'd break Devin's heart, and my own, if it meant saving him from Zoran. I hated what I had to do, but there was no other choice. I took a sip of my tea. It had a strange, bitter taste to it.

"Is this just normal tea or some kind of witch's brew?" I asked, my voice as bitter as the drink in my hands.

"It's normal tea—with a little something added," my mother confessed. "Something to calm the nerves and bring you clarity."

"Right, well, next time you decide to drug me, can you warn me in advance?" I didn't mean to sound so ungrateful. Why was it every time I thought I'd found happiness the rug got pulled out from under me? How much could one person take before completely giving up and breaking apart?

"I did not drug you," my mother protested.

"Never mind about that. I need to find Kees, and ask him if he'll agree to be my pretend boyfriend." I almost choked on the words.

"I know where the boy lives, but I doubt he'd be home at this hour. I can take you to him later this evening if you'd like."

Reluctantly, I agreed to meet my mother later, happy for a few hours of delay. With nothing else to do, I returned home, while Rayden went to his shop. I tried distracting myself by reading, but I was too anxious to focus.

I was still in a foul mood when my mother showed up later. "I came to check on you," she said. "How are you holding up?"

I shook my head. "It's hard for me to believe any of this is happening. First Dad, then Kate, and now I have to give up Devin on top of everything else. Why do I keep losing the people I love?"

With no answers to give, all my mother could do was wrap her arms around me and let me sob into her shoulder.

"Did you manage to talk to Kees?" I asked after a few minutes, drying my eyes at the same time.

"No. As expected, he wasn't home, but I left a message with his mother letting him know I wanted to talk to him about something."

Before I could reply, there was a knock on the door.

"Who is it?" my mother called out.

"Devin."

I shook my head, but didn't say a word, hoping my mother would figure out what I needed her to do without me asking.

She got up to answer the door, opening it only wide enough to stick her head out and say, "Lilli isn't feeling well, Devin. She's in bed right now."

I couldn't hear his response.

When they were done talking my mother closed the door and turned toward me putting a finger over her lips before mouthing the words, "Wait 'til he's gone."

A few minutes passed, and then my mother walked over to me. "He said to tell you he loves you."

I let out the breath I'd been holding. My mother sat beside me brushing my hair over my shoulder. "Are you okay?" she asked.

I shook my head but couldn't bring myself to actually speak.

My mother stood. "Perhaps it's best if I give you some space."

I nodded, grateful that she knew what I needed without me having to tell her.

"Will you be all right?"

I nodded again. My mother kissed the top of my head and then left while I sat there trying not to let my grief consume me.

Chapter 12

I was a mess inside the next morning when Devin showed up.

"I have something for you," he said after greeting me with a kiss.

"What is it?"

He handed me a small satchel. From it I pulled out a shiny dagger with a steel blade and intricately carved gold handle.

"Whatever happened to flowers or chocolate?" I asked, in a feeble attempt at humor.

"Neither will protect your life, and besides, I can get you those things anytime.

"Right." I walked over to the table and placed the dagger down on it, not really wanting to think about a time or situation I'd need to use it. "Thanks, I guess."

Devin rested a hand on top of mine. "I know you can't imagine ever using it, and you may never have to, but with everything that's going on, I'd feel better if you kept this with you at all times. Just in case."

"We've already been over this. Zoran is not going to hurt me."

"He won't, but that doesn't mean one of his newfound demon friends won't. They're sinister creatures, Lilli. With no loyalty to anyone but themselves."

I was tired of thinking about my father and demons and dark magic. "Can we talk about something else for a change?" We were running out of time and I wanted to savor every last second I had with him instead of thinking about fighting off demons. Except I couldn't tell Devin that, because he was blissfully unaware of what I was still working up the courage to tell him. "Like breakfast. Have you had anything to eat yet?"

"I want you to be prepared for what might be coming, Lilli, that's all," Devin said, ignoring my question.

I pulled my hand away from his and walked over to the kitchen area to grab some cups and plates.

"Is something wrong?" Devin asked eyeing me. "You're acting . . . strange."

I shook my head. "I have no idea what you're talking about."

"If something was going on, you'd tell me, right? No keeping secrets?"

"Of course not," I said, I feeling the blood drain from my face and hoping Devin wouldn't notice.

"I have news."

I glanced over my shoulder. "What kind of news?"

"My father has helped me find the perfect plot of land for our future home, and we've made sure no one else has a claim to it," he said. "I want to show it to you first, though. If you like it, my father has promised to help me build our house. It won't be very big, at least not at first, but it will be ours."

His news should've sent my heart racing, instead it felt like a knife in my gut. I looked away from him.

"About that . . ." Before I could finish my thought, a sudden eerie feeling that the two of us were no longer alone came over me. I turned around and sucked in a frightened breath. A few feet behind Devin stood Zoran. His long dark hair hung loose casting shadows over his face. He looked as menacing and fierce as the first time I'd met him.

I glanced at Devin, who was staring at Zoran with a startled look on his face. Before he could say or do anything, with a flick of his hand, Zoran sent him flying across the room.

"What is he doing here?" Zoran hissed as he walked over to me, his eyes blazing.

"I'm not the only one who lives here, you know," I said, looking at Devin out of the corner of my eye. He was trying to get back on his feet. "My cousin is Devin's best friend."

"You're the one who shouldn't be here," Devin said, staggering a little as he moved toward us. "Lilli wants nothing to do with you."

"I'm her father, half-breed. She *owes* me her love and loyalty."

"After everything you've done, I don't owe you anything." I practically spat those words at Zoran.

"You were supposed to have ended things with that animal," he said, cocking his head toward Devin.

Devin took a step closer, his jaw and fists clenched. I needed to keep him from doing anything stupid. As quickly as I could, I reached into my mind searching for the most peaceful thoughts I could muster, even though my head was filled with chaos. But somehow, when you are faced with difficult choices, you find a way to make things happen you never imagined possible. I cast my feelings of peace and tranquility outward, praying they were enough to keep Devin calm so that he wouldn't go after Zoran, whom he didn't have a prayer of defeating.

"I was going to," I said while trying to maintain my concentration. "As a matter of fact, I was just about to tell Devin to leave me alone before you barged in here unannounced and unwelcome."

Devin turned to look at me, a placid but puzzled expression on his face. "What did you just say?"

"Well, tell him already," Zoran demanded. "Tell him that a half-breed like him isn't worthy of a powerful witch whose father will soon be ruler of this world and beyond."

A feeling of dread came over me. Before I could ask Zoran what he meant by that, I heard a scraping sound coming from the table and turned my head to see what was causing it. The dagger Devin had just given me was being dragged telekinetically across the table. A moment later, it sailed through the air, stopping right in front of Devin.

"Tell him to leave, to get out and never come back, or I will slice him until he bleeds out on the floor in front of you."

"Stop it!"

Devin's shoulders moved as if he was trying to lift his arms and reach for the dagger, but he couldn't. Zoran's magic was pinning Devin's arms to his sides. Yet despite the dagger hovering in front of him and his lack of mobility, his expression remained calm even as he backed away. The dagger followed him.

"You won't be able to get away," Zoran said, laughing mirthfully.

"Stop it!" I exclaimed again, barely able to get the words out over the lump of fear and misery caught in my throat. I ran to Devin's side, feeling my concentration waning. His expression had morphed from peaceful to angry. I glared at Zoran. "I already told you I'd end things with Devin. You promised you'd leave him alone in exchange."

"But I'm the one holding all the cards, daughter. If I kill him, I get what I want. Sparing him assures me nothing."

"If you kill him, I will never forgive you. I will hate you until the last day of my life. Is that really what you want?"

Zoran let out a deep breath. "Very well." The dagger fell to the ground in front of Devin. I stared at it for a moment before bending down at the same time as Devin to pick it up.

"Let me have it," he whispered.

I shook my head. I knew what Devin was thinking, but it was too risky. He had the speed and reflexes of a shapeshifter, but Zoran wasn't stupid, and his telekinetic powers gave him a huge advantage.

"I'm sorry, it has to be this way, Devin." This time, I spoke loud enough for Zoran to hear. "But we both know it can never work between us."

Devin straightened up slowly, and then I did the same, my hand gripped firmly around the handle of the dagger. He looked at me quizzically. I suspected he knew I was only saying those words to appease Zoran and was trying to figure out whether or not he was supposed to be playing along.

"Fine," Devin mumbled. "If that's what you want, then I'll leave." He leaned in to whisper, "I'll be back. We'll figure this out together."

Then he walked away from me, past Zoran, sparing me a quick glance over his shoulder before closing the front door behind him.

"Are you satisfied?" I asked. "Did it feel good to watch me be cruel?"

Zoran laughed. "If that's what you consider cruel, then I'm afraid you have a lot to learn."

"Those aren't the kinds of lessons I'm interested in."

"If your plan is to try and trick me and run into that half-breed's arms the minute I leave, think again," Zoran warned. "Know that at any moment in time I may be watching you, just as I've been watching your mother. And it will be that way until the two of you have earned my trust."

"What are you even doing here? Haven't you got more important things to do than worry about my love life?"

"You're my daughter. Every aspect of your life concerns me," Zoran replied. "But you're right. This time I didn't come to discuss the half-breed. I came to tell you that my plan is reaching its final stages. Once the Council and their Messengers have surrendered to me and the Wilds is mine, I would like my wife and daughter to rule beside me willingly."

"You know that's never going to happen."

Zoran shrugged. "Your choice. But know this. If you won't give me your allegiance and love freely, I'll take it any way I can get it."

"How can you expect that I could ever love you after everything you've done?"

"You've never even given me a chance. I know I've made mistakes, but it was your mother's lies that led me down that path. Let me make things up to you. I can give you everything your heart has ever desired."

"My heart desires Devin," I said hoping the desperation in my voice would sway him.

Zoran took a few steps closer, reaching for me, but I backed away, refusing to let him touch me. "I can find you a match far more suitable than that creature."

I shook my head. There was no point in arguing. "You should go. Devin has probably already alerted the Council that you're here. Any second now, they'll be knocking down the door to get to you."

Zoran laughed. "They're already outside, trying desperately to figure out a way to breech the wards I placed on this home before entering it today. But they'll fail because they are cowards, too afraid of using dark magic even though any other kind is no match for me."

I ran to the window. True to his word, several Council members and Messengers were outside, but every time one of them took a step closer to Rayden's home, their body was flung away by some invisible force that kept them from getting any closer. I watched for another stunned moment, the gravity of situation sinking in, until I felt a hand on my shoulder.

"There is a place for you by my side, Lilli. You just have to accept it." Zoran leaned in closer and whispered into my ear, "There is no other choice."

He vanished after that, leaving me alone with my fear and despair.

Chapter 13

Syre was the first to burst inside. Whatever magical ward Zoran had placed around Rayden's home must have vanished along with him.

"Where is he?" Syre demanded as several other Council members rushed in behind him.

"He's gone," I said.

Syre began reciting some sort of incantation. I assumed he was trying to pick up on the magical trace teleporting left behind in the hope of tracking Zoran down.

"There's nothing. No trace at all," Syre said, turning to address his fellow Council members. They seemed shocked, but it came as no surprise to me at all. Zoran always thought ahead. He was undefeatable.

"Did you really think he'd risk showing up here if he thought any of you could follow him? You all raised him, you should know he's smarter than that."

"What did he tell you?" Marus asked, peering over Syre's shoulder at me.

"That he plans on ruling in your place with me and my

mother by his side."

"The perfect family," Sana muttered. "It's what he's always wanted ever since his father died."

"We did our best to give it to him," Tibor said, putting a hand on Sana's shoulder.

"There's no point in rehashing all of that," Marus said, "We need to return to the compound and come up with a way to find Zoran before we run out of time."

I gritted my teeth and refrained from saying what I really wanted to, which was that they were already out of time. I didn't know much about magic, but from where I stood, it seemed like Zoran was unstoppable.

"You go on," Syre said. "I need to talk to Lilli first, and then I'll follow."

One by one the Council members disappeared leaving me alone with their leader. I turned my back to him. He put his hand on my shoulder. "Are you all right, child?" he asked.

"No." I shook my head. "I'm not."

"What happened here?"

"He was about to kill Devin." When Syre glanced at my hand, I realized I still held the dagger in my hand. I walked over to the table and laid it down. "As if he hasn't already taken so much from me already."

"What do you mean by that?"

"I . . . I went to visit my aunt," I said, suddenly wishing I hadn't brought it up. I doubted Syre would be pleased that I'd teleported into my aunt's garage just because I couldn't bring myself to break up with Devin face to face. "She had no idea who I was, though. All her memories of me are gone thanks to Zoran."

"What makes you think it was Zoran?"

"Who else would hurt me like that?"

Syre sighed and shook his head. "I'm very sorry for everything you've had to endure in your short life," he said, bowing his head as if afraid to meet my gaze. "And while I agree that your father has done many awful things, erasing Kate's memories wasn't one of them."

I crossed my arms. "And how would you know that?"

He lifted his head and fixed his steely eyes on me. "It was us, the Council, we are the ones who erased Kate's memories."

My mouth opened, then closed. I was too stunned to speak.

"It was a difficult choice, but one we all agreed was for the best," Syre said. "The concept of greater good has always been hard for humans to understand. You were raised amongst them, so you are not accustomed to making sacrifices to protect your fellow witches."

"How is erasing my aunt's memories supposed to protect witches?" I said, trying not to stumble over my words. "And since when did you determine that you have the right to decide what is best for me?"

"The Council's decisions are not based on what we think is best for you or anyone else, but what's best for *all* of witchkind," he replied. "Every trip back and forth from here to the human world invites questions and suspicion. You made a decision to live here, which, given your ability, was a wise one. It is time you realize that you cannot live your life in two worlds. *This* is the world you belong to. The woman you call Aunt Kate is not even a true blood relative. We understand you care for her, but too much of a risk existed that eventually she would have questions for you that our laws forbid you to answer. This way she suspects nothing, our existence remains the secret it must be, and Kate feels no pain. There's no loss in her heart. We erased her memories as a kindness to her, and believe it or not, to you as well."

His attempt to placate me only made me angrier. Fury washed over me like a wave dragging me away from the shore. I imagined my anger as something real, something tangible. A bow and arrow. Pulling the arrow back first, I let it fly across the room and watched in my mind as it sailed in Syre's direction. He staggered backwards and clutched at his chest.

Just then, my mother ran into the house. "I heard what happened." She glanced back and forth between me and Syre. "Lilli, what are you doing?"

"Hurting him the way he hurt me," I replied my voice full of the satisfaction I felt.

"It's not him you're upset with, Lilli. Don't take your anger for Zoran out on Syre."

"You're wrong, Mother. I'm upset with him, too," I said, trying very hard not to cry. "He's the one who took Kate's memories. Not Zoran."

My mother walked over to me and grabbed my hand. "Syre is a very old witch, Lilli. He can't take too much more of what you're doing to him. I know you're angry, but you have to let it go."

I glanced at Syre, who had gone quite pale, and though I didn't want her to be, I realized my mother was right. Punishing him wouldn't bring my aunt's memories back.

I snatched my toxic emotions back. "You had no right!" I shouted at Syre.

He lowered his hand from his chest and took a few calming breaths before replying, "As the head of the Council, I take full responsibility. Our job requires us to make hard decisions sometimes, Lilli. I realize we have caused you pain, but it is our responsibility to decide what is the greater good. One day you will understand."

"No." I shook my head. "I will never understand, because it didn't have to be this way. If you didn't want me leaving the Wilds, you could've just said so."

Syre lowered himself onto the couch. He leaned forward resting his elbows on his knees. "You are right," he said. "Some of us assumed you wouldn't return to your childhood home and, therefore, would never find out what was done to your aunt, but I knew different. After it was done, I was filled with regret, which is the reason I stayed behind just now after the others left. I wanted to confess what we'd done and apologize."

"You're apologizing?" I could hardly believe it. "Do you really think saying sorry will fix what you've done?"

Syre shook his head. "Of course not. This isn't the way I wanted things to happen, but you must understand that even though I am the leader of the Council, decisions are still made by a majority of votes."

"So you're saying it wasn't your idea to erase my aunt's memories?"

"I shouldn't be telling you this."

"Syre, my daughter has been through so much over the past few days. Perhaps now isn't the time . . ."

"I understand. But before I leave, there is one more thing we must discuss. Please don't think me unsympathetic, but if we are to succeed in defeating Zoran, there is no time to waste. Things may look hopeless to you now, Lilli, but I don't believe that's the case. I know Zoran and the way he thinks. As his power grows, so will his confidence, and that's what will ultimately cause his downfall."

"And if you're wrong?"

"Then the Wilds will become a very dark place, and when it does, I have no idea what will happen as witches search for an escape from his tyranny."

"There has to be something we can do," I said.

Syre frowned. "I have an idea, but I'm afraid neither of you will like it."

"Who cares if we like it, so long as it works?" my mother said.

I waited for Syre to tell us what he had up his sleeve, but he remained silent, staring at me and my mother, studying our expressions.

"Well, are you going to tell us your great idea or not?" I asked, impatiently.

"It will require a strength I'm not sure you have, dear child."

"First of all, I'm eighteen, which means you can stop calling me child. And second of all, I have nothing left to lose, which means I'll do whatever it takes."

"Very well," Syre said. "You'll need to find a way to make Zoran trust you. And you, Naiara, will need to do the same. Is that something you are capable of after everything he's put you through?"

I felt the blood drain from my face.

"I've done it once before," my mother said. "Which means I can surely do it again."

"I can, too," I said. "I'll do whatever I have to."

"I fear that asking this of the two of you will tempt you to turn down that same dark path Zoran chose."

I swallowed hard. Had Syre reached into my mind and read my thoughts? Had he known that from the moment I'd looked out of the window earlier and seen what Zoran's magic had done that I'd wanted a bit of that power for myself? If I had it, I could find a way to get Zoran out of my life and keep the people I loved safe.

"I'm not like Zoran," I said, trying as much to convince myself as Syre. I refused to believe I could take after my father.

"I know you're not. But fear and heartache have a way of making us lose our way."

"That won't happen. I know what's at stake."

"Good." Syre lifted his hand to stroke his beard. "In order to make this work, neither of you can be in direct contact with us. Summon a Messenger only as a last resort. If you have news of Zoran, it must be transmitted to me telepathically."

"I will need to help Lilli practice using that ability."

Back when Devin and I were on the run from Zoran, Devin had tried to teach me how to connect with my mother telepathically, but it wasn't until I was stuck in the Void that I'd actually been able to do it. I hadn't realized I could communicate with anyone other than my mother that way. "I can do it, I know I can."

"You must convince your father that your relationship with Devin is really and truly over and that you've realized he was all wrong for you. If Zoran has even the smallest suspicion you're not being sincere, you will be right back where you started. All ground you might have gained will vanish. It is imperative that you do not let this happen, because the only way Zoran will share his secrets with you is if you convince him you've forgiven him and want to give him a chance to be a father to you."

"If that's what it takes," I said, ignoring the churning in my stomach.

"Then I will take my leave." Syre stood and crossed the room.

As he reached for the doorknob, I said, "You know, none of us would be in this situation now if you'd stepped in sooner instead of letting Zoran get away with so much for so long."

Syre turned back to me. "If a bad temper and jealous disposition were crimes, half of witchkind would be locked up on Bloodstone Island."

"If my mother had come to you and told you about her vision, the one of Zoran trying to kill me, would you have tried to stop him?"

Syre finally seemed to get my point. "The Council's job has always been to protect witches from the dangers of dark magic and demons and to keep our kind from being discovered by humans. To do this we have many rules we expect witches to follow. The problem is witches are a wild people, we always have been. The risk with too many restrictions is that all of them will be ignored. That is why it was decided long ago that it wasn't the Council's place to involve themselves in personal problems."

"So it would have been perfectly fine with you if Zoran had killed me the way my mother believed he would?" I demanded.

"Even if we'd been inclined to step in and offer you protection, would it have changed anything?"

"I . . . suppose not," I said, realizing what he was getting at.

There was no undoing something that had been prophesied to happen. My mother had tried and failed.

"I will leave you with these parting words, Lilli. Be wise and be careful," Syre said before turning back around to open the door and make his exit.

Chapter 14

Neither crying nor freaking out was going to help me, I reminded myself after Syre left. Instead I took a deep breath and gathered my thoughts.

"So what now?" I asked my mother.

"I was able to speak to Kees earlier and let him know you wanted to discuss something with him. He should be here shortly."

My eyes fluttered shut for a second. The pounding in my head made it hard to think straight. I'd almost forgot all about Kees, and wasn't exactly thrilled with the reminder. Not that it mattered.

"How does Zoran do it?" I said, still stunned by what had just taken place in my own home. "How does he watch me when he's not around?"

"I could be wrong about this. There's no telling what kinds of magic he's fooling around with these days, but I suspect he's using his specter."

"What's a specter?"

My mother shook her head. "I forget how much you still have

to learn," she said. "A specter is a spirit that all witches have inside of them. We can learn to control this spirit and send it long distances to do our bidding without anyone ever knowing because specters are invisible."

"Are you serious?" I said, incredulous. "So you're saying that at any moment in time Zoran could be sending some invisible spirit out to spy on me?"

"Yes," my mother replied. "That's exactly right."

"That must be how he knew I hadn't broken up with Devin."

"I should've realized that's what he was doing much sooner," my mother said. "Never mind that it's forbidden and that most witches have no idea how to do that kind of magic anymore. Your father must've been taught by someone, and we all know he has no regard for rules. From now on we'll have to be much more careful if we are to succeed with the task Syre gave us."

My mother walked over to the table and picked up the dagger. She placed it in the sheath Devin had brought along with it and carried it over to me.

"I want you to have this with you at all times," she said.

I took it from her even though the last thing I ever pictured myself doing was using it. I bent, lifted my pants leg, and strapped it to my calf.

"Lilli, listen to me. We have to assume that at any moment in time Zoran may be watching and listening. He most likely isn't right now, since he's only just left. Once Kees arrives we will tell him our plan, but from then on we must speak and behave as we would if Zoran was in the room with us."

"That's just great," I mumbled, trying not to give in to that helpless feeling I felt taking over.

Try not to worry.

I heard her voice in my head. I was about to respond out loud when I realized that was wrong. If I replied aloud to anything my mother said to me telepathically, Zoran would realize what we were up to.

My mother took my hand. "You have a soft heart. I know hurting Devin's feelings must've been hard for you, even if it was for the best."

I nodded. "You're right," I said, going along with her. "I know it's for the best."

Before my mother could reply, there was a knock on the door.

"That must be Kees," she said.

I went to open the door and let him in.

"What a nice surprise," I said, giving him the best smile I could manage under the circumstances. "I didn't expect another visit from you so soon."

Kees frowned. "Your mother told me you wanted to speak to me."

Whisper in his ear. Ask him to create one of his illusions so it appears that we are saying one thing when we are actually saying another.

I leaned in closer to him and whispered the words my mother had just spoken in my head even though I wasn't entirely sure what she meant by them.

"Yes, I do," I said, trying to act as normally as one could given the circumstances. "It's been such a strange day that I almost forgot."

"She takes after her mother. I'm always forgetting things."

Kees turned his head, only now noticing that my mother was

in the room. "Hello, Naiara." He glanced back and forth between the two of us. "Do you mind telling me what's going on?"

"Only if you're sure that no one but the three of us will hear what's being said," my mother replied.

"I've taken care of Lilli's request."

"Oh good." My mother smiled. "In that case why don't you and Lilli take a seat while I make us some tea."

"Well, start talking," Kees said as the two of us sat down.

"My mother thinks Zoran is using his specter to spy on me. And, well let's just put it this way, there are things I preferred he didn't hear me say."

"That's not a problem," Kees said. "Perhaps from now on when you need me to create an illusion for you a signal would be best."

"I can clench my hands together like this," I said lacing my fingers together and holding them on my lap in front of me."

"That should work."

My mother walked over to us with three cups of steaming hot tea on a tray. She handed a cup to Kees first, then me, before sitting down. "Before we discuss this further, I have one question for you, Kees," my mother said. "How do we know whether or not we can truly trust you? You helped Zoran once. What's to keep you from helping him again?"

"That was before I realized how evil he really is," Kees said. He turned his head in my direction. "I thought all he planned on doing with you was giving you a terrible fright. I had no idea he was going to force me to help him summon a demon."

"If I find out you are betraying my daughter, I will kill you myself," my mother said.

"Mother!"

"It's okay," Kees said. "I understand her reluctance to trust me, I really do."

"Asking him here was your idea and Rayden's."

"I know. And I do think we can trust Kees. But just in case I want to make it clear from the beginning what his betrayal will cost."

"There's no need for warnings," Kees said. "If there is something I can do to help Lilli, I will."

"Good," my mother said glancing at me. "Should I tell him what we need or do you prefer to explain?"

"It should be me," I said despite knowing how awkward of a conversation this was going to be. I sat there for a moment trying to figure out how to put everything into words before blurting out, "I need you to pretend you have feelings for me."

"Why do you need me to do that?"

"It's kind of a long story, but basically, Zoran doesn't want me with Devin, so I need to convince Devin that I don't love him anymore. Which is where you come in. The only way to keep Devin safe is to convince him that I've fallen in love with someone else."

"And that someone else is supposed to be me?"

"Yes."

"You do know what will happen to me if Zoran finds out I'm helping you to deceive him?" he said. "And Devin will be furious. I saw the look in his eye at the weapons shop the other day. I think you did, too."

"You're right. I'm sorry," I said, bowing my head. "I'll understand if you say no."

"I'm not saying no. I'm just trying to explain the way things are. This is a dangerous game you're asking me to play."

"These are dangerous times," my mother said. "You're being given a chance to make a difference, to make amends for the way you helped Zoran punish my daughter—"

"I know that, which is why my answer is yes." He turned toward me. "So we are to pretend we're in love, yes?"

I nodded.

"This is going to be interesting," he said with a roguish smile on his face.

"Thank you," I said, feeling partly relieved and partly sick to my stomach. Kees was handsome, and though I didn't know him well, he seemed kind, but he wasn't Devin. I didn't love him, and I had no idea how I was going to pretend that I did.

"Well, now that that's been settled, I will take my leave," my mother said, getting up from the couch. She walked over to me and gave me a kiss on the cheek. "We will talk again tomorrow."

I felt awkward sitting beside Kees after she left, though I supposed I'd need to get over that feeling if we were going to convince everyone we were growing close. "So what now?"

"That's up to you," Kees replied. "This was your idea, after all."

I thought for a minute. "When you ran into me and Devin in the weapons shop it was because he was showing me around the Markets. I haven't had a chance to see much of the Wilds since I arrived a few weeks ago. Maybe you can continue where Devin left off."

"That's sound like fun. How about we meet here in the morning just after breakfast?"

"Okay."

Kees and I both stood. I stuck out my hand to shake on our deal. He looked down at it and frowned. "If we're pretending to fall in love, you're going to have to do better than that." He pulled me into a hug I hadn't seen coming.

My body tensed. I wasn't used to being touched by any other man besides Devin.

"I'm not going to bite, you know," Kees said, sensing my hesitation. He pulled away from me and tilted my chin up so I could look into his brilliant blue eyes.

"Of course. I know that." I turned my head. "It's just that, even though we're only pretending, I still feel like I'm betraying Devin."

"He's lucky to have had you," Kees said, his eyes fluttered shut for a moment. I wondered if that meant he'd reached the end of how far he could keep his illusion in place.

I forced myself to smile, reminding myself that one only got good at something by practicing. I'd never been good at pretending, but there was too much on the line for me to let that stand in my way.

"I can't wait for tomorrow," I said, trying to sound petulant. "I'm tired of the way Devin has kept me cooped up in here."

Just as his name left my lips, Devin pushed the door open. He stood in the doorway staring at me and Kees in shocked silence for a moment before stalking across the room.

"What are you doing here?" I said.

Devin glanced at me for a moment and then turned his gaze to Kees, glaring at him. "The question isn't what I'm doing here." He grabbed Kees by the front of his shirt with a look of fury in his eyes I'd never seen before. "The question is, what the hell is he doing here?"

Chapter 15

I tried prying Devin and Kees apart, but both of them were too strong. "Kees is my friend. He can come visit me anytime he wants to," I said.

"Oh come on now. You didn't really think whatever you had with Lilli would last," Kees said, taunting Devin. "Did you?"

"Stop it," I hissed at Kees as he jerked away from Devin.

The angry look on Devin's face tore through me, but I knew I couldn't let it get to me. "What are you even doing here?" I asked, trying my best to sound impatient. "And what gives you the right to barge in without being invited?"

"I recognized his scent," Devin said, pointing to Kees. "After what just happened with Zoran, I was worried he was helping him again, and that you might be in danger."

"Except my father doesn't want to hurt me. You've said that before yourself," I said, "So even if Kees was helping him again, I wouldn't be in any danger."

"You haven't said what he's doing here."

"Because I don't owe you an explanation. Like I told you earlier, it's over between us."

Devin's eyes darted back and forth between me and Kees. "Right. You said that when Zoran was here." He backed away from me. "I get it."

From the way he said it I could tell he didn't. He was probably making all kinds of assumptions. Ones that were mostly right. My job was to convince him he was wrong, though. That this wasn't just an act. But now was not the time. Too much had already happened today, and I was thoroughly exhausted.

Devin glared at Kees before finally turning around and walking away. My knees felt weak as he closed the door behind himself. I took a step and almost stumbled over my feet, but Kees caught me before I fell.

"This isn't easy for you, is it?"

I leaned into him, resting my head against his shoulder as tears rolled down my cheeks, Kees just stood there quietly with one arm wrapped around me. "I shouldn't be doing this," I finally said. "We barely know each other."

"It's okay. I don't mind."

I pulled away from him and walked over to the window closest to me. With my arms folded across my chest, I just stood there staring outside. How could it look so peaceful out there when there was such a huge storm brewing inside of me? "Thank you for coming, and for agreeing to help," I said with my back turned to Kees. "But for now I'd like to be alone, if that's all right with you."

"Of course." Kees walked over to me and rested his hand on the small of my back. "I'll return in the morning just like we planned."

I nodded, and Kees turned to walk away. After he left, I collapsed on the couch. By the time Rayden returned later I was still there.

"I heard about Zoran's visit," he said, crossing the room to sit beside me. "Are you all right?"

"I will be," I said, pressing my palms to my forehead. "Who told you?"

"Devin. He also said that you told him you didn't want to be with him anymore. Except I don't think he really believes you meant it."

"Well, he's going to have to," I said, my voice hollow. "Because whether I want to admit it or not, my father is right. Devin and I aren't meant for each other."

Rayden frowned. "What are you saying?"

I couldn't communicate with him the same way I did with my mother. Rayden was a healer, he didn't have mental powers. But I couldn't very well tell him I didn't mean what I'd just said. I thought about writing it down, but there was no guarantee that was safe to do either. Perhaps I was being paranoid, but with so much on the line, I couldn't afford not to be.

"I'm saying that I'm finally starting to accept that life in the Wilds isn't the same as it is in Crescent City where I grew up. And since I have nothing to go back to over there, it's time I figure out how to make things work out for me here. Without Devin."

"I'm confused," Rayden said, furrowing his brows. "I thought—"

"You know what? I almost forgot to tell you that my mother needs more willow bark. She asked me earlier to tell you to bring her some."

"She needs it right now?"

"Yes. Her stomach has been bothering her." I wasn't even sure sending Rayden to my mother's house would be all that helpful since Zoran was keeping an eye on her, too. But even if she couldn't tell him what was happening, at least it would get Rayden to stop badgering me.

"Okay. But this conversation isn't over. We'll pick it back up when I return."

After he left, I went into the kitchen where I began to tackle a stack of dishes that needed washing. Anything to keep my mind off what was happening. I filled a basin with water that was kept in a large metal tub beside the kitchen area before adding soapvine, a plant that was used here for all kinds of washing. It smelled like a cross between lemon verbena and lavender.

I was only halfway through when Rayden returned.

"How is my mother doing? I asked, hesitantly.

"Fine now. But it's a good thing you remembered to tell me she needed the willow bark," he said with a knowing look.

With both of us now realizing we needed to be careful about what we said to each other, a heavy silence descended between us.

I continued my washing while Rayden made himself some tea. When I was done I wiped my hands dry and turned to face my cousin who was sitting at the dining table with a blank look on his face.

"So I was thinking, now that I won't be spending any more of my time with Devin, I'll need to do something to help pass the time," I said. "If it's not an inconvenience, maybe I can help out at your shop?"

"Actually it would be nice to have someone give me a hand," Rayden offered. "But are you sure you really want to? The stares and unwelcome questions will take a while to die down."

"Might as well get it over with," I mumbled, not too happy about that part. But helping Rayden would leave me with less time on my hands to worry and might even give me a chance to learn about the different herbs he sold.

"Can I start the day after tomorrow?" I asked, remembering that I was supposed to meet Kees in the morning.

"Of course." Rayden got up and walked over to me. He ruffled my hair with his hand before kissing my cheek. "You should get some sleep, Lilli. It's been a long day."

My cousin was right. I was so tired that I didn't even bother brushing my teeth before crawling into bed and falling into a deep sleep.

The next morning I woke up early. Sun streaked into my room. I looked out of the giant picture window beside my bed, and for a moment everything seemed perfect. But then yesterday's events came rushing back to me. They hadn't been a dream.

I dressed in a hurry and crept down the hall trying not to wake my cousin, but it was too late for that. After grabbing my cloak, I heard a voice behind me. "Where are you going?"

I turned and faced Rayden who was walking over to me. "You're not going to like this, but I need to see Devin." I wasn't sure exactly what time Kees was coming, but I figured if I wasn't back by the time he arrived, he'd wait for me.

He crossed his arms over his chest and frowned. "You're right, I'm not."

"It's not what you think," I said. "I haven't changed my mind about us not being right for each other, but now I need to convince him of that."

"Devin is stubborn. But a part of him had to have known the truth since the two of you met."

"Which is what?"

"That things in the Wilds will never change as much as he wants them to. He is what he is through no fault of his own, but that doesn't mean he shouldn't have known better than to think he had a right to you."

I swallowed back the anger that had begun to boil up inside me. Rayden didn't mean those words, I knew that, but still, I couldn't help but hate hearing them.

"I wish he would have told me the truth from the beginning."

"He probably thought, at least for a while, that the two of you would stay in the human world forever, where I take it the same rules don't apply."

"No, they don't," I said, suddenly wistful for that brief, but carefree, period of time Devin and I had together before life had gone completely crazy.

Rayden leaned forward to kiss my cheek. "Good luck," he whispered in my ear.

After arriving in front of Devin's home I took a deep breath, trying to fill myself with calming thoughts, but nothing seemed to help quell the panicky feeling in my chest. The idea of saying hurtful things to Devin filled me with dread. Still, I knew what had to be done, and I couldn't let my fear and anxiety get in the way.

Before I even had a chance to knock on his door, it flew open, and Devin pulled me inside. "I was hoping you'd come," he said, wrapping his arms around me.

Out of the corner of my eyes, I saw that Kileena was already up and in the kitchen making breakfast. She didn't greet me.

"I think it's better if we go somewhere so we can talk privately," I whispered.

"Yes, of course."

He reached for my hand, but I jerked it away and held it behind my back.

"I don't need your help teleporting. Just tell me where you'd like to go. I can get there on my own."

The look on Devin's face, a cross between confusion and sadness, made me ache inside. "How about the meadow?"

"Fine." I swallowed the lump in my throat, remembering what we had done the last time we'd been there together. I wondered if Zoran had watched. The thought made me feel sick. I closed my eyes and pictured the tree Devin and I had made love under.

As soon as I opened them again, Devin said, "Tell me what happened after I left you with Zoran yesterday. I need to know everything."

"I don't want to talk about Zoran," I said. "I want to talk about us."

Devin tilted his head and just stared at me for a moment like he was trying to read me. "We can't not talk about Zoran after what happened yesterday. I heard every word he said, and I remember everything even though you used your power to keep me calm. It worked, you know. If it hadn't been for you, I'd probably be dead now."

I looked away refusing to stare into Devin's impossibly beautiful eyes. "I know you're thinking I only told you it was over because my father had that dagger hovering in front of you, but you're wrong," I said. "Which is the reason I asked you here, so I could convince you of that."

Devin took a step closer to me. "Zoran isn't here. It's just the two of us, so you can quit this act of yours."

"This isn't an act. I really did mean what I said to you yesterday. We're not right for each other."

Devin narrowed his eyes. "So just like that, you've decided you don't want me anymore? Whatever happened to you swearing that you didn't care what people said?"

"I don't want to care, but it's time we faced reality."

"What reality is that?"

"That we're not meant for each other. We never were. Back in Crescent City when we first met we were both living a lie. I didn't know it at the time, but you did. You knew it all along, but you kept the truth from me."

"This isn't you talking, Lilli. It's Zoran."

"No, it's not," I insisted. "Think about it. Haven't I been distant for the past few days? Ever since you showed me around the Markets. I heard the whispers and saw the stares, and I realized I didn't like them one bit. Nor do I like you telling me who I can and can't be friends with."

"I have never done that."

"Yes you did. After Kees greeted me in the weapons shop. Or have you already forgotten?"

"Why would you want to be friends with someone who helped Zoran hurt you?"

"He's asked for my forgiveness and I've given it to him," I said. "Just like I've given him my friendship. Kees comes from a powerful family just like mine. He can teach me things you can't. If I want to spend time with him, you have no right to try to stop me."

Devin narrowed his eyes. "Who are you, and what have you done with my Lilli?"

I folded my arms over my chest. "She was never truly yours."

"I don't believe you," Devin said, starting for the first time to sound a bit unsure. "You're only trying to protect me. But I don't need you to. I can take care of myself."

"You don't get it. All my life I've wanted something better, something more. I wanted a family. I wanted two parents, just like everyone else had. And I wanted people to stop thinking I was odd and actually want to be my friend instead of only talking to me to be polite," I said, pouring my heart out. I'd heard once that a lie is easier to speak if there is some truth to it. Whoever had invented that saying was right. "I may still be angry with Zoran for everything he's done, but I've also come to realize that he can give me the things I've always wanted. He can give me anything, actually. You may not see it yet, but the Council doesn't stand a chance against him. Zoran will win, and when he does, he expects me to be his daughter. For all his flaws, Zoran loves me, he wants to be a father to me and to get to know me better, and I think it's about time I let him."

"What! After everything he's done to you?"

"He didn't know I was his daughter at the time. My mother shares the blame for what happened to me, and I've forgiven her."

"You can't be serious."

"I at least owe my father a chance," I said. "And I owe myself one, too. A chance to get to know the Wilds on my own terms, without you hovering over me and telling me what to do and think all the time like I'm a child. Because I'm not, you know. I'm a powerful witch, far more powerful than you, in fact."

"No. No." Devin shook his head. "I'm never going to accept this, Lilli." He took a step closer to me. I backed away. "What about our plans—the home I was going to build for us?"

"Find someone else to share it with," I said, even though the idea of Devin with another woman was almost physically painful. Without me wanting them to, tears formed in the corners of my eyes. I couldn't let Devin see me cry, or he'd realize everything I'd just told him was a lie. I turned my back to him. His hand on my shoulder startled me. But instead of turning around to face him, I jerked away, closed my eyes and teleported to my mother's home leaving him standing there in the meadow all alone with the disgusting words I'd just told him.

I pounded on her door until she answered. "You just came from talking to Devin, didn't you?" she said, immediately noticing my tear-stained cheeks.

I nodded. My mother slid her arm around my waist and ushered me inside. We sat at the table. "I know hurting his feelings must've been hard, but it was for the best. Zoran and I see eye to eye on basically nothing, but perhaps he was right about Devin not being the best match for you."

Before I could respond I heard her voice inside my head. *Don't forget. From now on this is how we speak to each other if we have something to say that needs to remain between the two of us.*

Having her communicate telepathically with me was still so unnerving.

"I was so sure I loved him," I said. "And I didn't want to admit that Zoran might actually be right."

"That's always how it is between fathers and daughters."

"Was that how it was with your father?" I knew next to nothing about my mother's parents other than that they no longer lived in the Wilds. They worked as some sort of magical ambassadors and lived amongst the fairies. My mother didn't have a good relationship with either of them, so their absence suited her just fine.

"Yes, very much so. I remember when I told him I didn't want to marry Zoran. He laughed and told me I'd lost my mind. Not too much longer after that, I decided to run away."

"Where do you suppose Zoran is right now?" I asked, changing the subject.

"No doubt he's in the Underworld."

Why can't the Council track him down if they know where he is?

The Underworld is vast, and Zoran is most likely being protected by powerful demons. It would be a suicide mission for the Council to search for him there. They'll have to wait until he makes another appearance here.

"I wonder when he'll come visit me again," I said, out loud this time.

"That is something I'm sure only your father knows." My mother put her hand on my knee. "Enough about that. Have you had breakfast? I can make you something if you're hungry."

I shook my head. "Actually, I should get going. I'm supposed to meet Kees this morning." I stood and headed for the door.

"Promise me you'll be careful," my mother called out after me.

"I will be," I said, although, truthfully, without Devin nothing seemed to matter. I had to keep reminding myself that our separation was temporary. But what if it wasn't? What if I'd done such a good job of chasing him away that I'd chased him right into someone else's arms? The thought made me sick to my stomach.

Kees knocked on my door a few minutes after I returned home. I let him inside. "Are you ready?" he asked.

"I guess I am."

"Well, come then." He took my hand and led me outside. From there we teleported back to the Markets where I'd run into him only a few days earlier. Somehow, it felt like a lifetime. How could so much have happened in so little time? I'd lost Kate for good, broken up with Devin, and agreed to play spy for the Council, whom I hated, so I could stop my maniac of a father.

Kees and I headed down the walkway in front of the shops, strolling beside each other. He explained what was in each store. Not that I couldn't figure it out on my own, but I didn't bother telling Kees that. We passed a few clothing shops, a bookstore, and another that sold furniture. I spotted the weapons store from the other day and thought about the dagger Devin had bought me. It was strapped to my leg, not because I planned on using it, but because both he and my mother insisted I carry it on me at all times and something in my head told me to heed their words.

After we wound our way around the circular walkway, I noticed a path leading away from the town center. The stretch of road was mostly deserted, but I noticed a two-story cottage a little ways off.

"What's in there?" I asked Kees.

"Oh, that's nothing but a dusty old library. Hardly anyone ever uses it."

Despite Kees's obvious lack of enthusiasm, my curiosity was piqued. "Can we check it out?"

He shrugged. "Sure, if you really want to."

Inside there was no one manning a check-out desk.

"There's no one here. What happens if someone wants to check out a book?"

Kees seemed confused by my question so I explained how libraries in the human world worked. "The library staff is supposed to make sure whoever borrows a book returns it."

"We don't have much of a problem with thievery in the Wilds," Kees said. "Anyone who wants to borrow a book, simply comes in here anytime they want, finds the book they are looking for, and returns it when they are finished with it."

There wasn't a huge selection of books, but a few caught my eye, and I skimmed through their pages. Kees seemed totally bored, so I returned the book I was looking through to its space on the shelf and made a mental note to return another day to explore further.

"Would you like to get some lunch?" Kees asked as we headed back.

I'd skipped breakfast and had begun to feel hunger pangs, so lunch sounded perfect.

Kees took me to Tabitha's. I was hesitant about returning since I'd only just had lunch with Devin there a few days ago.

"Is something wrong?" Kees asked, sensing my reluctance.

I shook my head. "No, nothing." I was too hungry to be picky and Devin had said Tabitha's was the best place to eat in the Wilds.

A few minutes after we seated ourselves, Tabitha walked up to our table.

"Back again," she said. "I take it that means you must've enjoyed your meal."

"I didn't realize you'd been here before," Kees said.

"Yes, she was," Tabitha interjected. "It was just a few days ago, in fact. Except she was accompanied by someone else then. You know Devin, don't you, Kees?"

"Um, not very well."

"And he doesn't mind you bringing his lady to lunch?"

My face flushed. "First of all, Devin and I are not together. At least not anymore," I said. "And second of all, it's not your business who I have lunch with."

"Yes, well, you've put me in my place, haven't you? Raeburns have always been exceptionally good at doing that."

"Tabitha, that's enough," Kees said. "We came in here to eat, not to gossip."

"Then I should tell you what's on the menu today," she replied with a forced smile.

I let Kees decide for me what to eat. As Tabitha walked away, I stared at her back, tempted to run after her and ask her what the hell her problem was. She seemed so nice the other day. I decided not to let it bother me. Perhaps she was just having a bad day. Although I couldn't help but wonder what she'd meant by saying that Raeburns were good at putting people in their place.

Curiosity got the better of me so I asked Kees, "What do you think Tabitha meant by what she said about Raeburns?"

"Your father comes from a family of powerful witches. You've seen for yourself what he can do. He's an exceptionally skillful telekinetic," Kees explained. "And neither he nor anyone else in his family has ever been shy about letting others know how special they are."

"Does Zoran have a big family?" I knew his father was dead, and his mother mentally unstable as a result, but I hadn't ever asked about other relatives.

"He has no brothers or sisters, but he does have an aunt, an uncle and a cousin. Thankfully, they are not quite as haughty as he is, but they aren't what I would call humble, either."

"Do you think they will want to meet me?"

Kees shrugged. "I doubt it. Zoran mentioned they don't speak. Apparently, they didn't approve of his marriage to Naiara and that caused a huge rift."

Just then our meals appeared on our plates. I took a bite of fish, happy that at least Zoran's family was one problem I wouldn't have to deal with for now.

Chapter 16

The next day, Rayden and I left for his shop together. He gave me a more in-depth tour this time, showing me where jars and extra inventory were kept and how to use the scale for weighing customers' purchases. Then he flipped the sign in the window to *Open*. For the first hour the shop was mostly empty, but as the day wore on, it became busier and busier with far more customers than I remembered seeing the other day when I'd come with Devin.

"You've been very good for business," Rayden told me. "People have been in and out of here over the past few days hoping to catch a glimpse of you, but now that you're actually here, I can't believe the crowds."

"Great. That's all I need," I grumbled. "You couldn't have warned me?"

"It's got to be better than staying home all day driving yourself crazy with all those thoughts in your head."

He had a point. Any kind of distraction was better than sitting home alone brooding about Devin. At night, alone in my bed, all I could think about was how broken he had looked after what I'd told him in the meadow the other day. The only thing that stopped me from getting out of bed, running to him, and telling him it had all been a lie was the memory of Zoran hovering my dagger in front of him, ready to plunge it into his heart.

Yet even here, in the company of my cousin and his customers, I found myself preoccupied much of the time. So much so that sometimes it took asking me the same question several times before I realized I was being spoken to. This did nothing to quell the stares I received, not to mention the whispers. If it bothered Rayden, he didn't say anything about it. Instead he patiently instructed me on what he needed me to do. Thankfully, labeling and refilling jars didn't take much concentration.

Just as I was getting into a rhythm, my cousin tapped my shoulder. "Looks like you've got a visitor, Lilli."

I turned to see Kees walking toward me. "How did you know I was here?" I asked him.

"You mentioned it yesterday," he said. "I was hoping you might want to have lunch with me again today."

I wasn't actually in the mood for eating, but when I glanced at Rayden I saw him nodding. "Go on," he said.

"You want Devin to know you meant it when you said you didn't love him anymore, don't you?" Kees said. "There's no better way to do that than by us being seen together in the busiest part of the Wilds. Word will get back to him."

"All right. I guess," I said, hesitantly. Pretending that Kees and I were getting close had been my idea, but when the news got back to Devin, it would gut him. I'd sworn to myself I'd never hurt him again, and here I was doing the exact thing I'd promised I never would.

Tabitha treated me the same strange way she had the day before, which did nothing to help my lack of appetite. I was poor company for Kees, who wound up doing most of the talking, but if it bothered him, he never said a word. When he walked me back to Rayden's shop, I was sure he'd be happy to rid himself of my melancholy, but instead he asked if I'd join him for lunch again the next day.

"Sure," I said feebly.

Kees leaned in and gave me a quick kiss on my cheek before vanishing. I turned and walked back inside my cousin's store.

For the next few days, life seemed rather mundane given every crazy thing that had recently happened. I still struggled to drag myself out of bed. Sometimes I'd wake to the sound of Devin and Rayden arguing about me. Devin's pleading words and angry exchanges with Rayden made me sick to my stomach. Not only had I broken Devin's heart, but I'd ruined his friendship with my cousin. I began putting my pillow over my head to drown out their voices whenever I heard the two of them arguing. I fought to keep myself from running down the hallway and in to Devin's arms. Every day without him left me feeling like I had broken bones that refused to heal, leaving me with pain that never went away.

Working at Rayden's shop turned out to be the distraction I'd hoped for. It was as busy as ever. I crawled a bit further out of my shell every day, introducing myself and even exchanging small talk with Rayden's customers. Most of them were outwardly respectful, commenting on how much I looked like my mother instead of asking prying questions like where I'd been for the past eighteen years, or if my sudden appearance in the Wilds had anything to do with the fact that my father was now a fugitive.

Kees took me to lunch at Tabitha's every afternoon. She continued to treat me with cold indifference. I was tempted to ask her why but decided I didn't actually want to know. Making friends now was probably a mistake anyway. With a possible war on the horizon, everyone I got close to was someone I might end up losing. I felt bad enough that I'd dragged Kees into my drama.

Despite my outward calm, a storm brewed inside me. Whenever Kees and I spent time together, he did most of the talking. More than once he had to repeat something he'd said because my mind was elsewhere. Eventually, he was able to pull me into conversation by asking questions about my life before coming to the Wilds. After a while I found myself enjoying the amazed reaction he gave me when I described something he'd never heard of before.

"I never thought I'd say this, but I think I'd like to see the human world one day."

"I'd offer to take you, but I'm not sure I could handle the memories a trip there would bring back," I said blankly.

Kees dropped his fork and stared across the table at me. "It was careless of me to bring it up."

"I'm not glass, you know. You don't have to be so careful with what you say around me."

"I feel like I do because you always seem so sad."

"Really?" I looked down. "I thought I was doing a better job of hiding it."

Kees shook his head. "You seem more and more miserable every day."

"I'm sorry. I know hanging out with me must be a real drag."

He cocked an eyebrow. "A drag?"

I often forgot that some of the expressions familiar to me did not exist in the Wilds. After explaining to Kees what I meant, he smiled and said, "You're not a drag, but I am worried that if you don't try a bit harder to smile every now and then Zoran will believe it's because you're pining over Devin."

"Why should that matter?" I snapped. "He got what he wanted. Devin and I aren't together. Why do I have to pretend I'm happy about it on top of everything else?"

"Because that's the only way you're going to earn your father's trust," Kees said. "There's a big difference between following your father's wishes begrudgingly and following them because you are finally beginning to see he might be right about a thing or two."

"I know. I know. But I've never been good at pretending."

Kees reached across the table for my hand, and I immediately tensed. "Why don't you start by trying not to act like my touch disgusts you?"

"I do not act like that," I protested, before realizing Kees had a point. I didn't find him the least bit disgusting. He'd been nothing but kind to me, but I couldn't stop feeling like spending time with him meant I was betraying Devin.

"Okay. Maybe I'm exaggerating a bit," he said, smiling.

I smiled back and reminded myself that he was only trying to help, just like he had in the Void, even though he was almost as scared of Zoran as I was.

All of a sudden, Kees sat up straight and pulled his hand away from mine. I turned to look over my shoulder, wondering what had startled him, and saw Devin stalking over to our table with his eyes fixed on us and his jaw clenched.

I stood up, readying myself to stop Devin before he could reach Kees.

"What are you doing here with him?" Devin asked.

"Not that it's any of your business, but we're having lunch."

"I saw him holding your hand."

Kees stood and edged closer to me putting his hand on my shoulder. "You don't answer to him," he told me.

Devin pushed Kees's hand away. "Unless you want to lose that hand you better not even think about touching her again." He grabbed me and tried to pull me along with him, but I pulled away.

"I'm not going anywhere with you."

"This has been going on long enough," he said angrily.

I could feel people's eyes on us, staring, wondering what was going on. "Devin, you should go. This isn't the place for this."

"I've been told that you've been spending time with Kees and that the two of you come here for lunch practically every day, but I didn't believe it. Because you wouldn't hurt me like that. Then Rayden . . . *Rayden,* my best friend, told me to come here and see for myself." Devin shook his head. "Why are you with him?"

"That's not a question you have the right to ask me."

"You don't mean what you're saying," he said, his voice cracking. "You just needed a little space because things were moving too quickly and because of Zoran. I get it, that's why I've stayed away these past few days, but I can't do this anymore, Lilli. I can't be away from you. It's killing me. That can't be what you want."

"She does mean it," Kees said.

Devin shoved Kees, who stumbled back a step but remained upright. "Stay out of this."

"Kees is right," I said, stepping in between the two of them again. "I meant what I said when I told you we can't be together."

"Lilli, no." Devin tried to reach for me, but I backed away. His expression changed. Anger replaced the pain and confusion that had been there a moment ago. "You made me a promise. You said you wanted to spend the rest of your life with me." He reached into his pocket and then held out his hand so I could see the ring that rested in his palm. "It's why I got this for you."

My heart shattered. I felt the blood drain from my face. But I had no other choice than to reach out and close his hand around the ring. "You have to stop this, Devin. You're embarrassing yourself," I whispered.

"I don't care." Devin shook his head. "You think I don't know what this is about, but I do. I'm not scared of Zoran—"

"This isn't about Zoran," I said, moving closer to Kees. He clasped my hand in his. Instead of pulling it away, I gripped it tighter. "Kees and I have been getting to know each other. We're just better suited for each other than you and I ever were."

"You're killing me," Devin said. "Do you realize that's what you're doing? You are literally taking a knife and twisting it inside me until I die from the pain. And I don't understand why."

"Devin, that's enough." Tabitha, who'd been standing a few

feet away, walked over to the three of us. "You said what you came to say, and now it's time for you to go."

He turned around and glared at her. "I'm not going anywhere without Lilli."

Kees put his arm around me, and I buried my head in his chest. Looking at Devin, seeing him in pain like that, and knowing it was my fault, was too much for me.

"Can't you see she doesn't want to go anywhere with you," Tabitha said.

"Lilli." I looked up. Devin tried to move around Tabitha who was using her body to block him. "I won't give up on us. Not now, not ever. Do you hear me?"

I needed to do something before things got more out of hand. I pretended it was Devin's shirt, not Kees's, soaking up my tears. I flashed back to the first time Devin kissed me, and the time we spent together at the beach talking and lying beside each other listening to the waves crash into the shore. They were some of my happiest memories. I pictured myself shaping them into a giant ball, which I then hurled out over everyone inside the tavern because I was too crazed to focus on Devin alone.

Slowly the room filled with the sounds of lighthearted conversation. Contented expressions filled the faces of the people around me. Even Devin's. He wore the same smile he always did when we were together. I was the only one in pain now, but I swallowed it down, reminding myself that I couldn't let my concentration waver.

With everyone distracted by the blissful feelings I'd just given them, I snuck away, sparing only a quick glance over my shoulder as I walked outside. I closed my eyes as soon as I crossed the tavern's threshold, needing to be far away by the time my power over Tabitha's patrons waned. I pictured myself at my mother's home, and a moment later, I was. My mother opened the door at my knock.

"What happened?" she asked, leading me over to the couch.

I lay down and closed my eyes, too out of sorts to keep them open. A minute later, my mother placed a wet cloth over my forehead that smelled like it had been infused with mint. She sat beside me and stroked my hair with one of her hands. "Tell me everything," she commanded.

"That's why you almost passed out after you got here," my mother said when I finished explaining what had happened before I showed up on her doorstep. "It took a lot of magic for you to do what you did at Tabitha's, and then you teleported right over here. That's just too much magic all at once for someone who's not used to using it."

"I had no choice. You should have seen Devin."

You only took his pain away temporarily.

I couldn't stand seeing him that way.

You have to be easier on yourself, you're hurting, too.

The difference was that Devin's pain was my doing. Mine was Zoran's fault, which was why I couldn't stop feeling guilty about how I'd made Devin feel.

"Well, at least you finally got through to him," my mother said. "I'm sure Devin will leave you alone from now on."

"Yeah. I hope so," I said, playing along.

I managed to sit up. Just as I did someone started pounding on the door.

"I think I know who that is," my mother said, getting up.

Somehow, so did I. The idea of facing Devin again made me sick to my stomach.

"Open the door now, or I'll break it down," he shouted. I'd never heard him so angry.

"What do you want me to do?" my mother asked.

I stood and headed for the door without answering her. As soon as I opened it, Devin burst inside.

"Don't you ever do that to me again," he said, his eyes blazing. "Don't you ever use your magic to make me feel something that isn't real."

I didn't know what to say. My mother came to stand beside me. "She was just trying to keep things from getting out of hand."

"Things are already out of hand." Devin turned his head from my mother to me. "Take a good look at what you've done. You've broken me, Lilli. And no amount of magic will change that."

"I . . . I . . . I'm—"

"You're what, Lilli?" Devin's gaze felt like it was piercing me. "Don't tell me you're sorry, because I don't want your pity."

He turned away from me. Instinctively I reached out to grab his hand. The contact jolted me. My face flushed and my heart hammered. Devin glared at me over his shoulder, and I dropped his hand. He stormed away without another word, slamming the door shut on his way out. My strength went with him. Fearing I was about to collapse, I stumbled back to the couch, trying my best to hide the emotion overwhelming me.

It won't be like this forever. You will get him back.

I wanted to believe my mother was right, but I was already starting to lose hope.

Chapter 17

I spent the next few days in a haze-filled trance, nodding yes or no when people asked me questions, but not really saying much else. More than once, I caught the concerned looks my mother and Rayden exchanged. Thankfully, they kept their thoughts to themselves.

I barely paid attention to the lessons Rayden or my mother tried to give me. They seemed pointless. How would learning basic spells keep Zoran from destroying the future I'd hoped for since I was a child?

I also stopped going to lunch with Kees. After what had happened with Devin at Tabitha's, I couldn't bring myself to show my face there. Still, that didn't keep Kees from showing up every afternoon to ask if I'd changed my mind about accompanying him.

"Keep in mind, this moping of yours isn't doing much to convince anyone you've moved on from Devin," Kees said after I turned him down once again.

"He's right, you know," mumbled Rayden.

I glanced back and forth between the two of them before

hopping off my stool. "Fine. I won't be very good company, though."

"You've got some pretty powerful magic," Kees said as we walked together toward Tabitha's. "I don't remember ever feeling as happy as I did the other day when you used your ability. I never wanted it to stop."

Something suddenly occurred to me. "Zoran is immune to my powers now," I said. "And if he's immune to mine, why shouldn't he also be immune to yours?"

"Our situations are different. He's purposefully blocked your ability from affecting him because he expected you'd use your magic against him. I don't think it would occur to him that I'm using mine whenever the two of us talk."

"Why not? Zoran may be a lot of things, but he's not stupid."

"If your mother hadn't suggested I use my ability to conceal our conversations, I doubt I would have even considered doing something like this. This isn't how I normally use it, but your mother is quite clever."

"So you're sure he has no idea what we're talking about now?"

"Yes, I'm sure."

We walked inside the tavern and found a place to sit.

"I was wondering when I'd see the two of you again," Tabitha said as she walked over to our table. She turned her head toward me. "Are you doing all right?"

I managed a smile and nodded.

"Good. Now let's get some food in you before you wither away to nothing."

Tabitha's sudden attitude change had me puzzled. I wanted to ask her about it, but couldn't quite figure out how to. My chance came after we finished eating. Just as Kees laid the money to pay for our meal down on the table Tabitha walked over. "You're working at Rayden's shop, aren't you?"

I nodded.

"Can you come by after it closes?" she asked me. "There's something I'd like to talk to you about."

"Why can't you just tell me what you need to now?" I asked, suspicious.

"I know I've been a bit rude lately. I just want a chance to explain myself . . . privately."

"Okay. Well, I guess I'll see you later then."

Kees walked me back to Rayden's shop. This time, instead of the kiss on my cheek he usually gave me, Kees reached for my other hand, the one he wasn't already holding. "Have I ever told you how beautiful you are?" he said.

"Thank you." I looked away, the way he was staring into my eyes made me nervous.

"I wonder if Devin knew how lucky he was to have had you?" he asked.

"We were lucky to have each other," I said. "And yes, we both knew that."

"What I wouldn't give to have someone love me that way," he said wistfully.

"Someone will one day." I meant those words. Kees had a gentle soul. If there had never been a Devin, I could see myself one day falling for someone like Kees. But Devin had stolen my heart almost from the moment we met, and I'd never love anybody else the way I'd come to love him.

Kees dropped one of my hands and reached around the nape

of my neck to pull me closer to him. He pressed his lips on mine, but only for a moment. Relief ran through me that he hadn't tried for a longer kiss. I knew it was all part of our act, since we were supposed to be growing closer with each passing day, but that didn't change the fact that the only one I wanted kissing me was Devin. I looked to my right, then my left. There were enough people milling about that someone must've noticed the kiss. I wondered how long it would take for the news to reach Devin and what his reaction would be.

"Thank you for letting me take you to lunch."

"I'm the one who should be thanking you," I said. "Not just for lunch, either. But for everything else."

"Tomorrow instead of just lunch, can we spend the entire day together? There are still so many places in the Wilds I haven't gotten a chance to show you."

"I don't know. I'm supposed to be helping Rayden." I looked over my shoulder at my cousin, who was so busy he probably hadn't even noticed that Kees and I were standing right outside the door.

"I'm sure he won't mind if you take one day off."

"Hmmm. I guess you're right."

"It's settled then," Kees said, a smile spreading across his face. "I'll see you tomorrow morning."

I turned and walked inside Rayden's shop. Later that afternoon, I returned to Tabitha's She looked busy, and I considered telling her I'd just come another time, but I was too curious about what she wanted. I walked up to her instead. She glanced at me over her shoulder and said, "Let me go look for my brother. He can help out up here."

I didn't even know she had a brother, but a few minutes after she walked through the doors that led to the kitchen she returned with him beside her. "Lilli, this is my brother, Elyas. Elyas, this is Lilli."

He took my hand and kissed it. "A pleasure," he said. "You're even more beautiful than my sister described. Now I know why you have two men fighting over you."

My face heated at his remark.

"Ely has a tendency to say whatever comes into his head." She glared at him. "No matter how inappropriate it is."

Before I had a chance to reply, Tabitha took my hand. "C'mon," she said. "We'll talk outside, away from prying ears."

We walked quietly beside each other for a few minutes. I had no idea where she was taking me, but I followed anyway. We walked until the Markets were behind us and then down a gravel path that led into the woods.

"Did you realize I've known both Kees and Devin since we were kids?" she finally asked.

I shook my head.

"I consider both of them friends," she said. "And even though you and I don't know each other all that well, I'd like to consider you a friend, too."

Unsure of how to respond the only thing I could think to say was, "Thank you. I'd like that, too."

"About what happened the other day," she said. "I want you to know I'm not going to be taking sides."

"What do you mean by that?"

"Devin asked me to stop serving Kees. He said Kees stole you from him and had no honor, and if I couldn't see that, it meant I had none, either."

I let out a deep sigh. "This whole thing is one giant mess. I'm sorry you're involved at all. I had no idea Devin would show up while Kees and I were in the middle of lunch."

"Don't take this the wrong way, but I'm kind of wondering something," Tabitha said. "What made you fall in love with Devin in the first place? He's hardly suitable for someone like you."

I bit my tongue to keep from telling Tabitha what I thought about her words. She didn't know any better than to believe what almost every other witch in the Wilds did: that a half-breed like Devin had no business being with a witch from a powerful family like mine. "I didn't know anything about witches or shape-shifters when the two of us first met."

"He is handsome, I'll give you that. I can see how you fell in love with him."

Her words awakened a jealousy in me I'd never felt in my entire life. "There's a lot more to Devin than the way he looks," I snapped.

Tabitha stopped walking. "I knew it," she said.

"You knew what?"

"You still love him."

Fear prompted me to grab Tabitha by her wrist and squeeze hard. What if Zoran was listening? "I do not, and if you really want to be my friend, then you'll never say those words again."

"I heard what Devin said the other day. He was going to ask you to be his wife. A love like that isn't something you can just turn on and off."

"I . . . I can't talk about this," I said, shaking my head. "I'm sorry."

"Do you know what people have been saying about Zoran?"

"Not really." Rayden and my mother had mentioned a few different things, but I wasn't sure if they were the same things Tabitha was referring to.

"They say he wants to declare himself king. That he wants all of us to bow down to him and bend to his will," Tabitha said frostily. "If he succeeds in coming into power, will I be forced to bow down to you as well?"

Our conversation had taken an unexpected turn. I wanted to tell Tabitha the truth, that I was nothing like my father, but I couldn't.

"Of course not. I would never expect you or anyone else to bow to me."

"I'm happy to hear that," she said.

We continued to walk, this time silently as I processed our conversation. "Can I ask you something?" I finally said. Tabitha nodded and I continued. "Is everyone in the Wilds scared of Zoran?"

"Not everyone. Some people have been waiting a long time for the changes they think he'll make. But I'm not one of them. I don't want the change he'll bring."

"Tabitha, be careful what you say out loud."

"I'm not afraid of him."

You should be, I felt like telling her. But I kept my mouth shut. "I'm sorry, but it's getting late. I should get going." I turned around to walk away.

"It was pretty amazing seeing your power in action the other day," Tabitha said to my back. "You should ask Rayden to tell you about mine after you get home. It might explain a thing or two."

I left without replying. By the time I arrived home I still hadn't made much sense of the conversation I'd just had.

"So what did Tabitha want?" Rayden asked after I closed the door behind myself.

"She wanted to talk about what happened between Kees and Devin at her tavern." I looked up at my cousin remembering the last thing Tabitha had said to me. "What is Tabitha's ability?"

"She can read people."

I frowned. "So she's a telepath?"

"Not exactly," Rayden said. "She can't read the exact thoughts in your head, but she gets general impressions. For example, if someone's smile is fake, she knows."

So that's why Tabitha had wanted to talk to me—and in private, away from Kees. She'd been testing me. And she wanted me to know. It was why she'd told me to ask Rayden about her power. "That must be so overwhelming for her, considering she's around people all day long."

"Like you, she has control over when to use her ability," Rayden said. "But in general I think Tabitha likes being able to read people and figure out whether or not she can trust them."

Her sudden shift in attitude suddenly made sense to me. She must've assumed the worst of me after seeing me with Devin then Kees only a few days later. It wasn't until the scene Devin made in her tavern that she decided to actually check what was going on in my head. I wondered how much she knew and hoped she had the sense to keep whatever she did to herself.

"Is it okay if I take a day off from the shop tomorrow?" I asked, changing the subject. "Kees asked me if I could spend the day with him and I said yes."

"It's fine. Just be careful. Okay?"

I nodded. "I will be."

The next morning Kees showed up about an hour after Rayden left for work. He looked really nice with his blond hair brushed back into a low ponytail. I walked outside with him.

"Can you tell me where we're going?" I asked as he reached for my hand.

"I remember you mentioning more than once how much you love the ocean, so that's where I'm taking you."

He grasped my hand, and I closed my eyes. When I opened them a moment later, we stood in the middle of a sandy shore. The beach was different than the ones I'd grown up going to in California. I was used to wide shorelines and rocky cliffs as opposed to the lush forest that started only a few feet back from where we were standing. The water was clearer and the sand almost white. I took off my shoes and marveled at how it felt like powder underneath my feet.

It was a gorgeous day. The sun sparkled like a jewel, and the sky was clear and almost cloudless, yet I had to bite my lower lip and blink my eyes to hold back tears. Looking out at the ocean made me think of Devin. The last few times I'd been to the beach, it had been with him, and I couldn't shake the image of us lying beside each other on the sand from my mind.

Kees pulled out a mat from the basket he'd brought with him and laid it down on the sand. For a few minutes we just sat there without saying a word. I looked over my shoulder at the woods behind us, marveling at how close it was to the shoreline.

"This beach is beautiful," I said, turning back to stare at the water.

It was a warm day, and I suddenly had the urge to dip my feet into the water. I stood. Kees reached for my hand.

"Where are you going?"

"To get my feet wet."

"Be careful. There are many creatures in these waters you've most likely never encountered in the human world."

I sat back down, suddenly intrigued. "What kinds of creatures?"

Kees shrugged. "There are mermaids, although they are rather shy so you most likely won't have any trouble with them. Kelpies and selkies are the ones you have to watch out for. They like to play tricks."

"What are kelpies and selkies?"

"They're sea creatures who take on different forms. Kelpies can either look like we do, or like a horse, and selkies like seals," he said as simply as if he were talking about dolphins or sea lions. I supposed that in the Wilds mermaids, kelpies and selkies weren't strange at all, but it was still hard for me to believe they existed anywhere but in fairytales.

I vaguely remembered reading about kelpies when I was younger, and how they lured people onto their backs so they could then run off into the water to drown their riders, but selkies I'd never heard of.

"It doesn't seem fair to have such a beautiful ocean if you can't get in and enjoy," I said wistfully. The waters were so calm, unlike the shores of the beaches I was used to, where a riptide or strong current could mean death just as easily as I supposed a kelpie could.

"You can get in, just be careful," Kees said. "I'd couldn't bear it if anything bad happened to you."

The water was too inviting for kelpies or selkies to frighten me away. I rolled my pants up as far as they would go, removed the sheath and dagger that were strapped around my calf, dropped them onto the sand, and walked into the water. As the warm water lapped at my feet, I felt the most peaceful I had since I'd told Devin we couldn't be together. I closed my eyes and tilted my head up so I could feel the sun on my face.

A few minutes later, I felt a hand on my shoulder. For a moment, I imagined it was Devin's and that we were back in Crescent City. But I knew it couldn't be him.

"Everything okay?" Kees asked.

"Yes," I murmured, "I'm fine."

"I have food in the basket. Why don't we eat?" Kees said, taking my hand and leading me back to the mat. From the basket he pulled out two sandwiches, a large flask and a few pieces of fruit, which he laid down in front of me.

As I ate, I felt Kees's eyes on me. After a while I began to feel self-conscious about it. "Why are you looking at me like that?" I finally asked.

"Has anyone ever told you how beautiful you are?"

He had, just the day before, but I didn't bother reminding him. "Devin used to," I said. "All the time."

"After your father is caught and sent to Bloodstone Island, will you run straight back to him?"

"If he'll still have me after all the terrible things I've said to him."

"It doesn't bother you that people will talk, wondering why

you're settling for him when you can have someone far more powerful and respected?"

"I don't care what anyone thinks," I said. "It doesn't matter to me."

"That's what you say now. But when the whispers get louder, when people can't stop looking at you every time you go somewhere with Devin, don't tell me it won't affect you at all."

"What point are you trying to make?" I asked.

"Just that maybe it would be easier for you to be with someone else," he said. "And not only that, if you and Devin were to have children, there's no telling what they would be like."

"I don't care about that, either."

"Most witches seek mates they know will pass on powerful magic to their future child."

I shrugged. "Maybe it's because I didn't grow up here, but it just doesn't matter to me. Sometimes I think all this power is more of a burden than anything else. Take my mother, for example. I would hate to be able to see the future and all the bad things that will happen, knowing there's nothing I can do to stop them from taking place."

"I suppose you have a point," he said, not really sounding convinced.

Even though I refused to admit it out loud, I saw Kees's side of things. Being with someone other than Devin would probably make life easier. I'd overheard several conversations in Rayden's shop about how relieved my family must be that I'd come to my senses about Devin. Kees was a much better match, people said amongst themselves, knowing I was only a few feet away and could probably hear every word. How torturous life had to be for

Devin now, since he could hear a thousand times better than I could. I imagined the things he probably heard people saying about him and how painful that had to be. He'd told me once it was the reason he'd left the Wilds, to get away from people's prejudices against him. Only now, because of me, things were way worse than they'd ever been.

"Why are people here so cruel?" I asked. My anger had risen as I thought about how unfair things were for Devin. "It isn't Devin's fault that his father was a shape-shifter. It's not like he asked for his mother to be raped."

Kees seemed to ponder my question. "I don't know. It's just always been this way. Witches have always thought of other magical creatures as beneath them because we are more human-like than any of them." He chuckled. "It's ironic when you think about it, since humans have never particularly liked our kind."

"If we all gave each other a chance, think about how less complicated life would be."

"I suppose. But witches are stubborn folk. Our minds are not easily changed."

Which was just one more reason why Zoran succeeding would be a disaster. If peoples' attitudes toward shape-shifters were bad now, they'd only be worse with Zoran in power. I shook my head, not even wanting to think of it.

I finished my sandwich, took a few sips of cider from the flask Kees had brought, and went back into the water, wading up to my knees. I wished I had a bathing suit with me so I could dive in, but I hadn't anticipated how warm and refreshing the water would be. The ocean back in Crescent City was practically ice cold even in the summer.

Kees and I didn't talk about Devin or Zoran for the rest of the afternoon. Instead we splashed around in the water for a bit and then took a long walk along the shore. As the sun started making its descent toward the horizon, Kees said, "As much as I'd like to stay here with you 'til nightfall, I'm expected at my uncle's house soon, which means I should return you home now." He held his hand out for me.

"You know what," I said. "I'd actually like to stay a little bit longer." I wasn't ready to leave the peacefulness the ocean air provided behind yet.

He frowned. "I don't like the idea of leaving you here alone. It's not the gentlemanly thing to do."

"I'm a big girl," I said. "You don't need to worry about me. I can take care of myself."

"If something happens to you . . ."

"Nothing will happen," I said. "I'll be careful, and I swear I won't go back into the water."

Kees folded his arms across his chest. "Nothing I say will change your mind, will it?"

"Nope."

He let out a deep sigh, leaned in to kiss my cheek, stared at me for a moment and then closed his eyes before vanishing.

After he left, I sat back down on the sand and looked out at the water, fighting my urge to jump in. Maybe having some mythical horse creature drag me to my death wasn't such a bad idea. At least then I wouldn't be hurting all the time the way I was now.

But so much was riding on me staying alive. Without my help, Zoran would destroy the Council and rule the Wilds. Then he'd use his newly acquired dark magic skills to turn my mother into some mindless woman who blindly worshipped him. I couldn't let that happen. No matter how miserable I felt, people needed me.

Remaining behind on the beach had been a bad idea. All time alone seemed to do for me these days was give me more chances to feel sorry for myself. I let out a deep sigh and closed my eyes, readying myself to return home. But before I could clear my mind enough to picture Rayden's cabin, I heard a voice coming from behind me.

Chapter 18

Recognizing the voice, I turned my head. My insides twisted at the sight of my father, and I fought the urge to say something that would betray my true feelings.

"I thought he'd never leave," Zoran said, sounding exasperated. "It's nearly impossible to get you alone these days."

"Why does it matter? I'm sure you're more than capable of getting rid of anyone you don't want around."

"That's true," he said with a smug smile. "But you wouldn't be very happy with my methods, and I haven't given up on proving that I want to be a father to you."

For a moment I was at a loss for words. But then I remembered what Syre had asked of me. "Well, thank you for that," I said.

Zoran took a few steps closer to me. I stopped myself from backing away.

"I was wondering when I'd see you again," I said.

"Have you missed me, child?"

I had to be careful. If I seemed too eager, Zoran would be suspicious. "It's hard to miss someone you haven't really been given the chance to know."

Zoran's expression softened. "Are you saying that's what you want?"

I swallowed back the bile in my throat. "All my life I've dreamed about what it would be like to have a big family. A mother and father, cousins, aunts, uncles. I was sure it wasn't possible. My mother was supposed to be dead. All I had was the man who raised me and his sister. But they're gone now," I said. "I'm not going to lie. I miss them. But I've been given a chance most people don't get. Don't misunderstand, I'm still angry with you for what you did to me, but I'm trying to put it out of my head and forgive you."

"Lilli, my child." Before I realized what was happening, Zoran embraced me. I stopped myself from pulling away, refusing to betray my true feelings, no matter how hard pretending was.

"Father," I said, trying to keep my voice from trembling.

Zoran dropped his arms from around me. "All we have to do is convince your mother to forgive me, and then the three of us can be the family you have always wanted," he said, brushing my hair out of my face with his hand.

"But how can we be? You're a fugitive. The Council is searching for you everywhere."

Zoran tilted his head back and laughed. "You think I'm scared of the Council? Before long they will be no more."

"What is that supposed to mean?" I asked, chilled by the tone of his voice. "What are you planning?"

His expression hardened, and his eyes narrowed as he studied me. "As much as I'd like to believe I can trust you, I'm not yet certain that I can."

"Who will I tell? I hate the Council as much as you do. Maybe even more."

"And why is that?"

I hesitated before explaining, figuring Zoran wouldn't be pleased at the mention of Kate, given whose sister she was. Somehow, I found a way to twist the story, telling Zoran that I'd hoped to run away from Devin by returning to the human world only to find that my aunt's memories of me had been erased.

"Then you see what I'm talking about," Zoran said. "The Council runs each and every one of our lives. They decide what is and isn't good for us. It's not right. We should get to decide for ourselves. They've convinced witchkind that dark magic is dangerous, that our powers need to be limited, but that's only because they don't want anything threatening their positions. But I'm planning to liberate our kind from their tyranny. Witches were given the ability to use magic for a reason. We shouldn't be confined by the Council's rules or anyone else's. What is the purpose of magic if not to get what one most desires?"

"And what is it that you most desire?" I asked.

"The same thing you said you wanted a moment ago. Family. My wife and my daughter at my side as I rule the Wilds and show my fellow witches what our true potential is," he said before lowering his gaze and staring into my eyes. "And I want humankind groveling at our feet."

"Why? Because my mother fell in love with one of their kind?"

"No," he said, barely hiding a grimace. "It's because of the way we've been treated by them. Humankind wanted us dead, but instead of showing them that they were beneath us, witches ran from their wretched non-magical world with our tails between our legs. A true leader would've put humans in their place long ago instead of forcing witches into hiding."

"So you want to declare war against the Council, their supporters, *and* humankind?"

"Do you doubt I can succeed?"

I turned my back to Zoran and wrapped my arms around myself, suddenly chilled down to my bones. "Do you know the kinds of weapons humans have? Things have changed since the time of the witch trials. Humans have guns, and bombs. A war between them and us could rage for years. People will die, lots of them. That can't really be what you want."

Zoran put his hands on my shoulders. I kept myself from cringing at his touch. "You only say that because you haven't seen the army I've amassed. Once humankind sees my power, they will surrender and fall in line. Then we will be free to cross between our worlds without having to hide what we are from anyone."

"Where is this army now?" I asked, turning back around.

"In the Underworld," Zoran said. "I can show you what I've been working on for these past weeks, if you like."

I wasn't sure I wanted to know, but what I wanted didn't matter. I *needed* to know. "How are you going to do that?"

"Take my hand," he said, holding it out to me.

Hesitantly, I reached for it and closed my eyes trying to calm my pounding heart. Where was he taking me, and what was I going to see when I got there?

Chapter 19

Even before I opened my eyes, I knew Zoran and I had arrived. The air around me felt different. Gone was the smell of the briny ocean air and the feel of the sun warming my skin. Instead, the smell of ash overwhelmed my senses.

"What is this place?" I asked, staring down from the tier on which I stood beside my father. Below us was a huge open area. Torches provided the only light. If not for them, we'd be cloaked in total darkness. Where Zoran had taken me reminded me of my time in the Void, a place that carried with it only bad memories.

"We are in the caverns of the Underworld."

"The Underworld?" I said as a slight shiver ran through me.

"Don't worry. You're perfectly safe here with me." Zoran cupped his hand around his mouth and shouted, "Assemble."

A moment later, I heard first a loud rumble and then the sound of hundreds of feet marching. Slowly, the space below us filled with what looked to be moving statues. The giant beasts walked on all fours.

"What are they?" I asked, almost too stunned to get the words out.

"Griffin gargoyles."

"They look like the statues at the Council's compound."

"These gargoyles work for me, though," Zoran replied proudly. "They are my army. Created by the use of pure dark magic."

"Created? By whom?" I asked.

"By myself and by my mentors who have so graciously agreed to teach me the type of magic the Council forbids us from learning."

"You mean demons? They're the ones teaching you, aren't they?"

"So what if they are? I'd be a fool not to glean knowledge from wherever I possibly can."

"Even I know that demons can't be trusted. Don't you remember the way Andras almost killed you after he thought you betrayed him?"

"Your concern is touching," Zoran said, steepling his fingers in front of him. "But I am not worried about being betrayed. My relationship with the greater demons who have been teaching me is a symbiotic one. Our army cannot be controlled without all of us working together, nor can we perform a shield spell without pooling our magic."

"What is a shield spell?" I asked, scared of the answer. I'd already learned far more than I'd wanted to.

"Perhaps it's better if you see for yourself." Zoran smiled and swept his arm out to his side while mumbling an incantation. "Try making those creatures feel something."

"How can I? They're not even alive."

"Of course they are." An impish smile spread across his face.

"You assumed they were objects, only moving because they'd been animated through magic. I'm surprised your mother and Rayden haven't done a better job of teaching you. Gargoyles are very much alive, just like you or I. They are typically used as guardians, sitting still as stone, but always watching, always keeping an eye out for any danger their masters might be in. And they have feelings, just like any other living creature."

"You want me use my ability on them?"

"Yes."

I had a sinking feeling that I wouldn't be able to, but out of morbid curiosity I tried anyway. I stared down at them, willing them to feel the same growing sense of despair and hopelessness I did. They did not react. If what my father had said was true, that gargoyles really did have feelings, then the shield spell he'd spoken of protected them from the effects of my magic. It was unbelievable. I couldn't imagine the power it must've taken to cast a spell like that over so many.

A million fears and doubts swirled around in my head. There was a lot I didn't know, but I was certain of one thing. The Council had no idea what they were up against. My father had an army that magic couldn't touch, and in the Wilds, magic was the strongest weapon. Without it, the Council was doomed. I swallowed the lump in my throat, refusing to show fear. "When are you planning on using them?"

"I have a few more pieces to put in place. A victory that doesn't include my child and wife by my side will be a hollow one." Zoran put his hand on my cheek. "I'm hoping that I truly have succeeded in proving to you how badly I want to be your father and how much I care for you."

I nodded, my tongue too tied to form words.

"Convincing your mother of my devotion will be far more difficult."

"And if you can't?"

"Like I told you before, I will take your devotion and hers any way I can get it. I prefer it to be given willingly, but if needed, I will use my power to bend her will."

"She regrets keeping us apart," I said. "She told me that the other day. I know she feels bad about lying to you for so many years. She only did it because she was scared."

"We shall see," he said.

I stared down at my father's dark army one more time. It seemed to me like he'd already won. What could the Council possibly do against this army of creatures?

"Don't you worry about what all this will cost you?" I asked in one last-ditch effort to get Zoran to see the error of his ways. If he was capable of love, that meant there had to be some good in him. "How could you even think of cooperating with demons when they're the ones who killed your father?"

"There is very little I won't do to get what I want. Even if it means working with the enemy."

"You can't trust demons. They may be your allies now, but don't think one, or even all of them, won't turn on you eventually. Especially if you don't do as they ask. Don't tell me you think answering to demons is better than answering to the Council?"

"Not unless I turn on them first," Zoran replied with self-assured smirk.

"I'm scared," I said, wrapping my arms around myself and lowering my head.

"You have no need to be. I know what I'm doing." Zoran lifted my chin with his fingertips. His piercing dark eyes stared into mine. "Listen to me, child. No one will hurt you, or your mother. Ever. They wouldn't dare try."

Another chill ran through me. "Can we leave this place? I . . . I don't like it here."

"Of course." Zoran draped his arm over my shoulder, and a moment later we were back on the beach where he'd found me earlier.

"Not a word of what I've shown you is to be shared with anyone," Zoran said. "Remember, I'm watching you, and if you betray me, I *will* know."

"Can I at least tell my mother that I saw you again?"

He nodded. "Give her a message from me. Tell her that despite her betrayal, I still love her."

And just like that, he vanished, leaving me alone to digest everything he'd just shown me.

Chapter 20

I wasn't sure if I should go straight to my mother's house or return home first. The only thing I was certain of was that Zoran would be watching to observe my reaction to everything he'd just shown me.

I decided the safest thing would be to go home and act like nothing had happened. Once there, I called out for my mother, connecting with her through the mental abilities we shared, and pleaded for her to come to me. She was the only one I could turn to because I had yet to figure out how to connect telepathically with Syre. Perhaps because he was just too far away.

"You're just in time for dinner," Rayden said as I walked inside. He was crouched down in front of the fireplace stirring the contents of a cast iron pot. "What were you and Kees up to all day?"

With still trembling hands I grabbed some bowls and spoons and began to set the table. "Kees took me to the beach."

"It's almost nightfall," he said. "Were you there the whole day?"

I nodded feebly.

"I expected you home earlier. I was starting to get worried about you."

A knock on the door interrupted my cousin's scolding, and I went to open it.

As my mother walked inside Rayden stood. "What a nice surprise," he said.

"I thought I'd surprise my daughter and my cousin. See how the two of you were doing." She glanced at the dining table. "But come to think of it, I am hungry. Would you mind if I stayed?"

"Of course not," Rayden replied, fetching another bowl and spoon and placing it on the table.

My mother kept glancing at me curiously, waiting for me to tell her why I'd asked her to come, but I wasn't sure where to begin. Then I remembered the message Zoran had given me for her.

"I saw Zoran today."

My mother's face blanched. "What did he want this time?"

"There's something he wants me to tell you."

My mother's face remained expressionless as I conveyed his message.

"Was that it?"

I shrugged. "Pretty much." *He also showed me his army. He's got hundreds of gargoyles ready to fight for him, and they're protected from magic by a shield spell he created with powerful demons.*

"It would be better for him to tell me himself," my mother replied. "I can't help but wonder why he hasn't tried to see me even once." *We must find a way to let the Council know as soon as possible.*

"Maybe he's worried that you're still angry at him for what

he tried to do to me in the Void." *What good will telling the Council do? And if Zoran finds out I breathed a word of his plan, he'll stop trusting me.* Not that I was sure he did now, but I didn't want to erase the little bit of progress I had made with him.

My mother sighed. "A great deal of that is my fault." *I will find a way for Syre to call on you since you're still not able to reach him yourself. He's a clever man, he won't do or say anything to let Zoran suspect you've betrayed him.*

"Did Zoran say anything else?" Rayden asked. "Did he tell you where he's been and what he's up to?"

I shook my head. "I think he doesn't want to involve me in whatever he's planning."

"It's better that way," my mother said.

"I agree," Rayden said. "And knowing Zoran, you're correct. He was always rather chivalrous when it came to you, Naiara. I suspect he'll be the same with Lilli. Whatever he's up to, he won't let anything happen to his wife or child."

As usual, Rayden's words were carefully chosen, as were mine and my mother's. I was so tired of having to be cautious about everything I said. It wore on me and after a while our charade of a dinner conversation grew wearisome.

"I need to wash all the sand off my body," I said, finding an excuse to get up from the table.

"You don't want any dessert?" Rayden asked. "I made a pigeonberry pie."

I loved anything with pigeonberries in them. The bright orange berries were the perfect mix of tart and sweet and were used to make jams and all kinds of desserts. They were a favorite food not just of witches, but of all kinds of animals, too, especially pigeons who could easily pluck them off the bushes they grew on. Normally I would have gladly had some of Rayden's pie, but the image of Zoran's gargoyle army still lingered in my mind, wiping away my appetite.

"No thank you. I think all that time in the sun today has worn me out."

I gave my mother a kiss on her cheek before heading down the hallway to my bedroom. After stripping off my clothes, I drew a bath, hoping it would help me relax, but it was impossible to erase Zoran's words from my head.

All night, I racked my brain trying to convince myself that things were not as bleak as they seemed. But how could they not be? Zoran's advantage seemed insurmountable. It wasn't until late in the night that I was finally able to sleep. By then, I'd resolved that the only thing for me to do was to wait to hear from Syre so I could tell him everything I'd seen, praying that he would have an idea of how to defeat an army of living stone creatures who were shielded from harm by dark magic.

Chapter 21

My mind continued to race all the next day. Working at the apothecary usually distracted me, but not now, not after what Zoran had shown me. I was so lost in thought that I told everyone who approached me with a question that they were better off asking Rayden, even though I'd become quite proficient at helping customers find what they were looking for.

One insistent man refused to accept my dismissiveness. "If I had a question for Rayden, I'd have asked him instead of you," he said.

"Rayden owns this shop, I'm just here helping," I replied, quite annoyed at how rude he was being.

"Then do your job and come and help me," he demanded.

I stopped myself from groaning and got off my stool. "What is it that you need?"

"An herb called moonflower." *And to know exactly what your father showed you yesterday.*

It was Syre's voice inside my head. Although I had no idea how that was possible since he was not in the shop with me. I did my best to keep myself from reacting.

"Moonflower?" I managed to squeak out.

It's a disguise, dear child.

It hadn't occurred to me that Syre could do something like that. I looked up at the man standing in front of me. Gone was the white beard and wrinkled face. In its place was a thick-waisted middle-aged man with brown eyes and hair.

Syre? A part of me worried I was being tricked.

Yes, it's me. Now be quick. Your mother told me about the gargoyles and the shield spell. Is there anything else I need to know?

I reached for a jar on from the shelf in front of me. "This is what you're looking for," I said, handing it to Syre. *Zoran doesn't only want the Wilds. He also wants back into the human world.*

"Ah yes. Thank you." He placed a few coins in my hand. "I need only an ounce."

"Of course." I turned to grab an empty jar from the work table. *If what you're telling me is true, then there is only one way to stop your father.*

And that would be?

He must be killed—and you must be the one to do it.

I nearly dropped the jar and its contents onto the work table in front of me. *Are you crazy? Why does it have to be me?*

You're the only one he'll let his guard down around.

And exactly how am I supposed to kill him?

"Thank you very much for this," Syre said as I handed him his purchase. *Poison will be easiest I suspect.* He turned to leave.

Where are you going?

There is much to do. No time to tarry here. Ask your cousin to help you with the ingredients. And do it fast, I sense we do not have much time.

He strode out of the store before I had a chance to say another word and vanished as soon as his feet crossed the threshold.

I hated all this cloak and dagger stuff. I didn't like not being able to speak freely or having to hide my feelings. Rayden stood only a few feet away, but I couldn't ask him for his thoughts or even tell him that Syre had just been in his shop.

I was so anxious to talk to someone about Zoran and about Syre's visit that by the time Kees came to take me for lunch, I practically leapt off my stool to join him.

When we got to Tabitha's tavern she came to take our lunch orders like she always did, except this time, before she walked away, I asked, "Can you sit with us for a few minutes?"

She looked at me quizzically, and then over her shoulder before saying, "I guess so."

I wasn't quite sure how to start the conversation so the three of us just sat there for a moment glancing at each other. "The other night when we spoke, were you testing me?" I finally asked.

"Testing you, why would I do that?" she replied, innocently.

"Everything you say right now is strictly between the three of us. Kees is using his power with illusions to change our words."

She glanced at Kees who gave a slight nod.

"Since that must take a great deal of concentration, I'll get straight to the point. Yes, Lilli. I was testing you. From the first time we met I had a good feeling about you. But with you being Zoran's daughter and all, I couldn't really be sure. And when you showed up here one day with Devin and the next with Kees, I became even less sure. I should've tried reading you then instead of assuming the worst," she said. "It wasn't until the other day, when Devin burst in here, I realized I'd been wrong to think so poorly of you. I could tell you didn't mean the things you were saying to him. That's why I decided it was time I figured you out once and for all. In these crazy times, it's important to know who your friends are and aren't."

"Working here, you must overhear lots of conversations. What are people saying about my father?"

"There's a growing divide here in the Wilds. A good number of us are tired of being made to feel we are inferior because of the family we were born into, and we're also tired of hearing that witches are somehow superior to every other being in the worlds. But a lot of witches think like your father does; they are doubtful of the Council's assertion that dark magic is far too dangerous to meddle with."

"So some people actually want my father to succeed?"

"Yes. Many witches, especially the ones from powerful families, feel like the restrictions the Council has placed on the use of dark magic are excessive. Zoran is hardly the first witch to feel that way, but he's the first to have made a move against the Council," Tabitha said. "I suspect learning that he had a daughter whom his wife hid from him amongst humans was the catalyst for thoughts that had been brewing in his head for quite some time."

"Tabitha is right," said Kees. "When Zoran first came to my father asking for help after he found out about you, he was enraged. He kept going on and on, saying what was the point of being given abilities you aren't permitted to use."

I furrowed my brows. "Your father?"

"Zoran and my father have been good friends since they were children. He asked my father to help him find you. My father offered me instead, telling Zoran I would do whatever was asked of me," Kees explained.

"Which begs the question, what makes you think you can trust Kees?" Tabitha asked, turning her head in his direction.

"I deeply regret helping Zoran, Lilli knows that," Kees said.

"You're not lying. But I can't help but wonder if your loyalty will remain with Lilli once you learn of her true feelings."

"True feelings about what?" I asked.

"That's not for me to say. That's between you and Kees and Devin."

I had no idea what she was talking about at first, but after a moment it dawned on me what she was hinting at. "Kees and I aren't really together. We're just pretending. But no one can know that, especially not Devin. He has to believe it's over between us because if Zoran suspects I still have feelings for Devin, he'll kill him. I can't let that happen."

"And you agreed to pretend to love Lilli?" Tabitha asked Kees. "That's a dangerous game you're playing. Wasn't it Naiara's deception that led Zoran down the dark path he's now on?"

"What is that supposed to mean?" I was confused, again.

"I know what you're trying to do, Lilli, but I'm worried about what the consequences of your actions will be. You saw Devin the other day. He was in pieces. I want to believe he's a better man than Zoran, but—"

"He is a better man than Zoran," I said emphatically. "He would never do the kinds of things Zoran has done."

"I hope you're right. I really do." Tabitha stood, shaking her head. "As much as I wish we could talk more, I've got to get back to work."

She put her hand on my shoulder before walking away.

It was impossible to eat after that. Guilt gnawed at my insides. What if Tabitha was right? What if Devin wound up letting that angry dark side we all had in us take over? What if he was tempted to use dark magic? Could he walk away from that kind of power, or would it take him over, like it had my father? *No way.* I'd sworn to Zoran once that Devin wasn't like him. I believed it then, and I still believed it now.

"I wonder why Tabitha feels the way she does about Zoran?" I said. "I imagine with her ability she must come from a respectable witch family."

"Long ago when witches and humans lived beside each other, some also fell in love, married, and had children together. Most witches have at least some human blood running through their veins. It's said the more powerful the witch, the less their blood has been tainted by humans. That's why families like yours and mine are held in higher regard. Tabitha's, however, is not." Kees took a sip of water from his cup before continuing. "People say her ability is just a watered-down version of telepathy."

"I can't believe humans are really that despicable to witches."

"They did torture, imprison and attempt to slaughter our kind."

"But that was hundreds of years ago."

"Witches have long memories. Perhaps because we live for so many more years than humans. Some people still have living grandparents that can tell them about those dark days. And some are still thirsty for revenge. People like Zoran," he lowered his voice, "and my parents."

"So all this time the Council has been the only thing standing between this revenge so many witches want?"

"Perhaps I'm being a tad overdramatic. Mostly talk of revenge is just that, talk. As much as some people want it, they don't actually want to lift a finger to make it happen. People may grumble, but most of us are content with our lives as they are. It's been a number of years since the last demon uprising. A lot of families lost loved ones during that time. A war, even a short-lived one, isn't something people are eager to undertake. But now that Zoran is out there somewhere, plotting to overthrow the Council, some witches are getting excited."

"But you're not one of those people?"

"To tell you the truth, I've never given much thought to humans until I met you. When we were in the Void and you talked about your aunt all I could think was that if you loved her as much as you said you did, she couldn't be as bad as witches often make humans out to be."

"People must realize that revenge comes with a price."

"I know. That's one thing I learned when Zoran forced me to help him summon that demon. Ever since that day, I've hated myself. Helping you is the only thing that frees me from that self-loathing."

I reached across the table for Kees's hand. I hadn't realized how hard he was being on himself. "I already told you that I forgave you."

The sound of door to the tavern being thrust open drowned out Kees's reply. I looked over my shoulder to see what all the fuss was about. A man had just burst inside, his face twisted in shock.

Tabitha, who was standing near the entrance, asked, "What's the matter?"

He turned to her and in a panicked voice said, "It came out of nowhere."

"What came out of nowhere?" she asked.

The color drained from the man's face. "The dead body that's lying out there by the fountain."

Chapter 22

Almost in unison, people got up from their tables and rushed outside to see what was going on. A large crowd had already gathered, making it impossible to see the body that was supposedly lying there.

"Back up," bellowed a man I couldn't see because he'd been swallowed by the crowd of people.

"What does the note say?" shouted a lady standing a few feet away from me.

"If you give me some space, I'll read it." The voice came from the same man who'd just ordered everyone to back up.

Slowly, people started to take a few steps away from where they'd just been craning their necks for a glimpse of the body. As they did, I saw it. Whoever lay there had the hood of a cloak pulled up, so I couldn't see if it was a man or woman. The man standing beside the body held a piece of paper in his hands. He crouched down and turned the body so the victim lay flat on the ground. Then he pulled the hood of the cloak back. I immediately recognized her face. By the reaction of the crowd I guessed most everyone else did too. It was Ina's, one of the Council members.

Her death, it seemed, had come in the most horrific way. There was a hole in the middle of her chest that was still smoking, the cloth around it burned. It was as if someone had set her heart on fire from inside her body. I could picture Ina's fear and the pain a death like that must've caused. I shuddered at the horror of it all. My father had done that. Sorrow, fear and disgust tore through me, but I grasped those feelings and shoved them away before I lost control.

"Soon you will have a new master," the man standing next to Ina's body began. His hands trembled ever so slightly as he read. "For those of you thinking of opposing me, consider this a warning. Be prepared to surrender to my will or face death."

People started talking amongst themselves while I just stood there in shock. Kees slid his hand around my waist. "Lilli, are you all right? Say something."

I turned to look at him. "I can't believe my father did this."

"He isn't himself anymore." He stared back at me grimly. "This is why the Council forbids dark magic. It destroys souls."

All of a sudden, I felt like I was going to be sick. I couldn't stand being anywhere near Ina's lifeless body for a second longer. I was afraid I'd lose control and that's the last thing I wanted to happen in a big crowd of people. Without a word of explanation to Kees I turned and ran. I ran past curious onlookers and empty stores, until I was back in the woods. I ran until my legs could no longer hold me. As I sank down onto my knees, tears streamed down my face. Zoran was going to win, and I would never get Devin back. I'd live the rest of my life with my mind under Zoran's control because there was no way I could keep this charade going for much longer. There was no way I could pretend to love a killer. Eventually, Zoran would realize I'd been faking. And then what would happen to me?

I wasn't sure how long I sat there, but eventually I heard someone rustling in the leaves behind me. I looked over my shoulder thinking that Kees had caught up to me. But it wasn't Kees. It was Rayden.

"How did you know I was here?"

"I saw you running and decided to follow."

"Rayden," I said, standing and drying my eyes with the back of my hands. "What are we going to do?"

He shook his head. "There aren't many good choices."

"From where I stand, there aren't any choices at all. Zoran has just shown everyone that he can get to the Council, that even they aren't safe from him. Ina's murder was a warning. It's what will happen to anyone who dares try to stop him."

"I'm afraid so." Rayden held his open arms out to me. As he embraced me, he also whispered in my ear. "You and Naiara are our only hope. You're the only ones who can get close enough to him to finish him off."

I did my best to keep my expression from reflecting how stunned those words had just left me. Had Rayden really just suggested what I thought he had? Did he know that it was what Syre has asked me to do only a few hours earlier? I took a step back from him, hoping to read something in his eyes that would answer my question.

"Come," he said, reaching for my hand. "Let's go back to the shop."

By the time we returned to the town center, Ina's body was gone, and so were the crowds it had attracted. For the next hour we had absolutely no customers. It seemed everyone had lost their interest in shopping, so after a while Rayden decided to close his shop early and the two of us headed back home. We arrived to find my mother outside waiting for us.

"I take it you heard what happened?" Rayden said.

"How could I not? It's all anyone's talking about," she said matter-of-factly. The tone of her voice surprised me. I expected her to both look and sound more upset. Often my mother wore her worry on her face, but she seemed remarkably placid given everything that had taken place.

"What I want to know is how Zoran managed to get Ina alone," Rayden said.

"He must've done something to lure her away from the compound," my mother replied. "But now that she's gone I doubt we'll ever find out what."

Rayden shook his head. "Let's go inside," he said, pulling his key from his pocket.

"What a strange day it's been," my mother said as she sat down. Again her voice was steady, not betraying a single ounce of the fear I was sure she had to be feeling.

"I'm not sure strange is the right word," I replied. *What are we going to do?*

"You're right, it's not." *There's nothing we can do. We have no choice but to wait and see how things play out.*

Rayden frowned. "You're not usually this calm about things."

"That's exactly what I was thinking," I said.

She gave us a weak smile. "I am, sometimes."

I couldn't help but wonder if she knew something and had just decided not to tell us. We glanced at each other wordlessly for a few moments before Rayden suggested dinner.

"A good hearty stew always makes things better," he said.

I nodded in agreement although I knew it would take more than stew to calm the fear that gnawed at my heart.

~

Despite the utter sense of dread I felt, I managed to face the next few days as if they were no different than any other. Strangely, my mother did the same. Her out-of-character calm continued, replacing her usual fretful personality. I couldn't shake the feeling that she knew something no one else did, but every time I pressed her for information, all she would say was, "You can't change what's destined, so what's the point in worrying?"

The day after Ina's body was dropped by the fountain, it rained for the first time since I'd arrived in the Wilds. It wasn't a normal kind of rain. The skies were gray, the wind howled, and the raindrops felt like little pin pricks as they landed on my skin. It was if Mother Nature herself was furious with what was happening.

But the weather wasn't the only strange thing to happen. Kees stopped showing up to take me for our afternoon lunch dates. I worried about what that meant. One afternoon I even asked Rayden if he could close his shop early and take me to Kees's house.

No one answered when I knocked on the door. Several more days passed, and still no Kees. I hadn't seen him since the day Ina had died, and I was seriously getting worried that something had happened to him.

There were no phones in the Wilds, so the only way to get a

hold of him was to send a letter, which wouldn't give me the immediate response I wanted, so I decided to look for him one more time. I was nervous as I knocked on his door. What if Zoran had somehow found out Kees was helping me to deceive him? I'd never forgive myself if Kees got hurt because of me. I had to make sure he was okay.

Chapter 23

It was strange the way homes were situated in the Wilds. There were no neighborhoods or street names; instead, homes were randomly scattered throughout the woods that covered much of the Wilds. Because witches mostly traveled by teleporting, I had no idea how far away Rayden's home was from my mother's or anyone else's.

Kees answered the door after a second round of knocking. I breathed a sigh of relief, thankful that he appeared completely fine. "Where have you been? How come you haven't been coming by the shop?" I asked.

Kees stared at me for a moment before lowering his head. "I'm not sure you want to know."

"Yes. I do," I said, frowning. I waited for him to look at me again before continuing. "We're friends," I said. "That means you can tell me anything, including what's going on with you."

He hesitated before replying. "If you really want to know, I'll tell you. But not here. Let's go somewhere else to talk."

I backed away as Kees walked outside, closing the door behind him. "Where do you want to go?"

"The beach," he said. "We had a good time there, and it's finally stopped raining."

I gave him my hand and shut my eyes.

Just like last time, there wasn't another soul in sight. And though the rain had stopped, the sand was still a bit wet. So instead of sitting down, Kees and I walked. "So now that we're here, are you going to tell me why you've been pulling a disappearing act?"

I waited for his explanation, but he remained silent.

"I think I know what's going on." I stopped walking and turned to face Kees. "I've been taking advantage of you, asking you to put yourself in danger. After what happened to Ina, I don't blame you if you're scared or if you've changed your mind about helping me."

He shook his head. "That's not it at all."

I stared at him inquisitively. "Then what's wrong?"

Kees took my hands in his and looked down, once more averting my gaze. He let out a deep breath and shook his head. "Do you remember the conversation we were having with Tabitha right before that man ran into the tavern yelling about a dead body?"

"Of course, how could I—"

The sound of someone clapping stopped me from finishing my sentence. Kees dropped my hands, and we both turned our heads to find Devin standing a few feet away with an angry smirk on his face. "Well, well, well, if isn't the happy couple."

My heart froze in my chest. "What are you doing here?" I asked.

"That isn't any of your concern," he snapped. "At least not anymore."

I suddenly realized what things must've looked like to Devin. The beach had been our special place, and here I was holding hands with Kees right in front of him. "Devin, it's not . . ." I stopped myself from continuing. It was better for him to keep thinking what he was thinking, no matter how painful it was for either of us.

"It's not what?" he asked. Instead of answering, I just stood there staring at him gape-mouthed.

"You know what, it doesn't matter," he finally said. "Nothing matters anymore."

"What is that supposed to mean?"

"I told you once there is no life for me without you in it. Do you remember that?" I nodded and Devin continued. "You might have not meant the things you said to me, but I did, every time."

Kees tugged on my hand. "C'mon, Lilli. We should go."

"No," I said leveling my gaze at Devin. "Not until he finishes explaining."

"Instead of wrapping my hands around his neck." Devin gestured toward Kees. "I've decided to get out of your way . . . permanently. He makes you happy and I love you too much to want anything for you other than that. You've made it clear that you've moved on, but I haven't, and I never will. There is no life for me without you in it."

"Would you get to the point already?" Kees said with a grim expression. "Neither of us has all day to listen to your self-pity."

"Don't push me, you lying dog," Devin snarled.

"Who are you calling a dog?"

"Stop it, you two." I glanced back and forth between Devin and Kees, waiting for them to cool off.

"Maybe *he's* too scared to try to stop Zoran," Devin said, pointing at Kees, "but there's no way I'm surrendering without a fight."

"Devin, you can't beat Zoran, he's too strong," I said.

"What should I do instead? Let him win? How do you think a half-breed like me will fare with him as our leader?"

"I won't let him hurt you."

He took a few steps toward me, stopping only inches away. My heart quickened. I clasped my hands together behind my back to keep myself from reaching for him. "Not even his daughter can protect me now. Not after what I've done."

"What have you done?"

"I've joined the Resistance. Better to die fighting than to die doing nothing."

"The Resistance?" I stammered. "What the hell is that?"

"Exactly what it sounds like. Shape-shifters and witches who know what life will be like with a dark witch like Zoran in power." Devin inclined his head and shrugged his shoulders. "Most of my fellow Resistance members think we stand a chance, but I know better. Fighting against Zoran is a suicide mission, but at least my life will have meant something."

"Devin, no." Without thinking I grabbed his hand. The contact sent an electric current through my body. "You can't do that. Zoran is more powerful than you can imagine. Anyone who even thinks of standing up to him will wind up just like Ina did."

He pulled his hand away from mine. It felt like a slap in my face. "Why do you care?"

"Just because we're not together, doesn't mean I want to see you dead," I replied angrily. I hadn't sacrificed my happiness, my heart, to wind up losing him in the end.

Kees stepped in between us and looked at Devin. "That's enough. If you feel like throwing away your life then so be it, but I won't let you make Lilli feel like your death is her fault. She deserves better than that from you."

"He even speaks for you now." Devin took a step back, his face twisted in an expression that was a cross between anger and sadness.

"Devin, it's not—" Before I could finish what I was going to say, he turned and sprinted away. I fought to keep myself from chasing after him. Not that it would make any difference. He was way faster than I'd ever be.

"Are you okay?" Kees asked.

I nodded and bit my lower lip, refusing to let myself cry despite the piercing pain in my heart.

Kees took my hand. "C'mon, let's sit down."

He took his jacket off and laid it down on the wet sand. For a moment I stood there staring in the direction Devin had just run, hoping to catch just one more glimpse of him, but he was long gone. I sat down and leaned into Kees as he wrapped his arm around my shoulders. I kept myself from crying, refusing to believe that Devin really meant what he said about joining the Resistance. Instead I stared at the water as the waves crashed against the shore. The recent stormy weather must've had an effect on the ocean, because it wasn't nearly as calm as it had been the last time Kees and I had been here.

"Lilli."

I looked up at him. "Yes?"

"Did I ever tell you you're the most beautiful woman I've ever seen?"

"Yes," I replied. "More than once, actually."

"I've thought that way from the moment Sabin brought you to the Wilds wearing those strange human clothes. What were those pants called again?"

"Jeans," I reminded him.

He smiled. "Oh yes, that's right."

He stared down at me for a moment before reaching around the back of my head, pulling me closer and pressing his lips on mine. It all happened so fast that it took me a moment to register what was happening. Kees, my friend, was kissing me.

I pulled away. "What are you doing?"

He stared at me with a mortified expression. "I . . . I'm sorry, I shouldn't have. It's just that you're sitting so close to me, and those eyes of yours, they're mesmerizing, and I've wanted to kiss you for so long. Even though you're still in love with Devin and probably always will be, I can't help the way I feel about you. I've been in love with you from the moment I first laid eyes on you, and I haven't been able to talk myself out of it, no matter how hard I've tried."

"Kees, I don't . . ." How had it never occurred to me that he had feelings for me? For weeks we'd been pretending, but I thought that's all it was. An act. I'd been buried so deep in my own heartache that I hadn't noticed.

"You don't what? Know what to say? Well, you don't have to, because nothing you do will make things better." He stood. "You wanted to know why I've been avoiding you. Well, now you know. I can't be around you anymore, Lilli. It's too hard. Tabitha was right the other day when she said we were playing a dangerous game. It wasn't your mother's deception that led your father down the dark path he's now on, but a broken heart, and I feel myself being pulled in that same direction. I want to break every rule for you so I can make you mine, no matter how wrong I know that is. When Devin just told you he was joining the Resistance, all I could think was that with him out of the way, maybe there would be a chance that one day you'd love me. But that's wrong, isn't it? Because if he died, it would break you, wouldn't it?"

I nodded, despite knowing the truth would hurt Kees. That was the last thing I wanted to do, but I couldn't lie to him. "Yes, it would."

He closed his eyes for a moment. "That's why I can't be around you anymore, Lilli."

I stood up and handed Kees his jacket. "I'm sorry, Kees. I had no idea. I really didn't. I never meant for this to happen."

For weeks we'd been pretending to have feelings for each other. It never occurred to me that for Kees it had been more than just an act. I felt awful that I'd put him in that position.

He managed a weak smile, though I could see the hurt in his eyes. "That's one of the things I love about you. You never *want* to hurt anyone. You've got such a kind and gentle soul. You're the opposite of your father. He's all darkness, and you're all light. I don't know how you do it."

I shook my head. "You're wrong about me." He didn't know that at that moment I was only thinking of myself and how I couldn't stand that I was losing him, too. I would never love him the way I loved Devin, but that didn't keep me from caring about him and hating that he was telling me goodbye.

He leaned forward and planted a kiss on my cheek. "I'm not wrong," he said before vanishing, leaving me alone, reeling from both his and Devin's revelations.

Chapter 24

After Kees left I just stood there staring out at the crashing waves trying to figure out what to do. There had to be a way to stop Devin from his suicide mission, but it was hard to think straight with Kees's words in my head. I hated that I'd hurt him.

Desperate for advice, I went to see my mother hoping she'd know what to do.

I knocked on her door.

"What's happened now?" she asked, after letting me in. Somehow she'd instantly recognizing the pained expression on my face.

"It's a long story." One I wasn't quite ready to tell. I needed a few minutes to pull my thoughts together first.

After my mother closed the door behind us, she pulled a chair from the table and set it beside another one that stood in front of the fireplace.

"Why are you sitting in front of the fire?" I asked taking a seat beside her.

She shivered. "It's just so cold."

I furrowed my brows. "Are you all right?" There was a slight chill in the air, but nothing that required a blazing fire.

"Zoran was here earlier," she replied, her voice hollow and the look in her eyes vacant.

My eyes opened wide. "What did he want?"

"To tell me that he still loves me and that he's forgiven me for keeping you from him." She turned her head from me and stared into the flames shooting up the chimney.

"And then what happened?"

"He kissed me," she said, her voice almost a whisper. I didn't need to ask her how she felt about it. It was obvious. For eighteen years my mother had played the role of the perfect dutiful wife in order to protect me, and she just couldn't do it anymore.

"Are you all right?" I asked, putting my hand on her shoulder.

"Of course I am," she said, glancing at me. "Why wouldn't I be?" *I will be.*

Can you do this? Can you really keep pretending that you love Zoran after everything he's done?

It was one thing for me to pretend. But for my mother things were different. A husband expected certain things from his wife.

She managed a weak smile. *It won't be for much longer. I can manage.*

I couldn't help but wonder what she meant by that. *Did you see something? Do you know something I don't?*

"Would you like some tea?" *You know I don't like to speak of my visions.*

"No, thank you." *If you know something, you have to tell me.*

All I can say is that whatever your father has planned will happen soon. Assuring himself that I still cared for him was his last step before he puts his plan in motion.

Before I could reply there was a knock on the door. My mother got up to answer it and let Rayden in. "What's the matter?" she asked him. I looked in their direction again, wondering why she had assumed something was wrong.

For a moment, it seemed like he was considering whether or not to speak. "Oh, what does it matter? I'm sure the news will reach Zoran's ears sooner or later anyway," he finally said, coming further into the room. "I overheard something today while I was closing up the shop. Apparently there's a group of witches going around calling themselves the Resistance. They plan on trying to kill Zoran after he gets the Council to surrender. And Devin has joined with them."

"I already know," I said, facing the fire once more, suddenly feeling the same chill my mother had complained about earlier. "I saw Devin earlier, and he told me all about it."

Rayden sat down beside me while my mother busied herself in the kitchen. "I've got to figure out a way to talk some sense into him."

"It won't make a difference," I said, knowing how stubborn Devin was.

"No," my mother agreed, "it won't."

"So what should we do?" Rayden said. "I can't just let my best friend die. We have to do something."

"Like what?" I said, frustrated. "Zoran has an army, and powers that no one even dreamed were possible. Anyone who tries to stop him will die."

"Except me and you," my mother said, walking over to us with two cups in her hands. She filled them with hot water from the kettle that sat on the floor beside the fireplace and handed one to Devin before taking a sip from the other. "Instead we'll have the pleasure of living the rest of our lives under his control."

"Death almost sounds better," I muttered.

"Don't say that," Rayden said. "As long as you are alive there is hope. Zoran's magic can be undone, but death can't be."

"It can only be undone if there is someone there to undo it," I replied. "Zoran won't leave anyone like that behind."

Rayden shook his head. "I just can't accept that this is the end of our way of life."

"We've been going about this the wrong way," I said. "Devin is the one who's on the right track. Instead of trying to outsmart Zoran we should be fighting against him."

"We won't win," my mother said.

"I broke Devin's heart for nothing," I said, as the realization of how everything was soon going to play out hit me. "I'm the reason he joined the Resistance."

"You are too quick to give up hope," my mother said. "And you're also not being careful. We could be heard."

"Does it really matter anymore?" I asked. The end was near, I could feel it. We had all hoped that Zoran would be captured by the Council, but we were fools to believe that's how things were going to turn out.

"Devin and I have been friends since we were children," Rayden said, "So I know him well enough to believe that without you in his life he has no problem dying along with anyone else brave or stupid enough to try to stop Zoran."

"You told me to give him up, you told me that was the only way to save him."

"I know I did, because back then I was sure the Council would find Zoran before long."

"Well, you were wrong."

"We all were," my mother said. "But not because we wanted to be."

"I know. I know you were only trying to protect Devin, and me. But it's too late for that. It's too late for everything."

"What are you saying?" Rayden asked.

"That I want to spend whatever time there is left with Devin. Even a few hours is better than nothing."

I ached for him now more than ever. Perhaps because seeing him earlier had awakened all those feelings I still had for him but had tried to bury. Or maybe it was because I couldn't shake the feeling that we were running out of time, that if I didn't find my way back to him now it would be too late.

My mother put her hands on my shoulders. She bent down and whispered in my ear, "Do what you must."

Chapter 25

The next morning I told Rayden I wasn't going to his shop with him. He didn't ask why. After he left I took a walk through the woods near the house. I'd woken up that morning with a sudden desire to savor each moment of my life before everything changed. As I stepped quietly between trees and over fallen branches, enjoying the way the gentle breeze felt on my skin and the scent of soil and pine, I thought about what I would say to Devin when I found him later.

My heart fluttered as I pictured myself in his arms, but then a terrible image pushed those thoughts away—Devin turning his back to me as my father appeared out of nowhere with a dagger in his hands. I sucked in a breath and clenched my trembling hands into fists.

I wound up taking a much longer walk than I'd planned. By the time I returned home, it was almost noon. I was surprised to find Rayden there.

"What are you doing here?" I asked.

"I had almost no customers all morning," Rayden replied. "More than half of the shops are closed. People are just too scared to go about their normal business. They know something is coming."

I'd noticed that, too. Ever since Ina's body had appeared, the crowd of shoppers had thinned.

"I hate having to just sit around and wait for whatever's coming," I said. "It makes me feel so helpless."

"Come sit next to me." Rayden patted the empty spot beside him on the couch. "There's something I need to tell you."

"What is it?"

"I've also decided to join the Resistance."

"You what?" I said. "Whatever happened to death being final, to not giving up hope?"

"I can't pretend not to hate Zoran and what he has done. Not just to you, but to Ina. I won't serve a ruler like that, which means I won't be spared. When Zoran sweeps through here, I'll die right along with everyone else who opposes him."

"Rayden, no—"

He held his hand up. "Let me finish." I nodded, and he continued. "There has never even been the smallest of chances that I would surrender, and I won't run. The Wilds is the only home I've ever known and I'm not interested in getting to know another. I truly thought the Council would find Zoran and that we'd all be safe and happy, but I was wrong. I may be your family, but I'm not Zoran's, so he has no reason to let me live. Not that I'd want to with him in power."

"I don't want to, either," I said, my voice cracking. "Which is why I want you to promise me something. Don't let Zoran take control of my mind. Promise me you'll take my life before he can do that."

"You don't know what you're asking. I love you, Lilli. And no matter how twisted Zoran's plan is, you won't be hurt. You'll live in the finest home and you won't want for anything."

"But I won't be me. What if Zoran makes me use my power to hurt other people? And what if on some level I know it? I don't want to spend the rest of my life feeling like I'm trapped in someone else's body."

Rayden looked away. "Okay," he said, his voice barely above a whisper. "I won't let it come to that, I swear."

I swallowed back the tears I felt forming and nodded. When the knot in my throat dissolved, I stood up and headed toward the door.

"Where are you going?"

I considered telling him I was going to see Devin. He hadn't seemed opposed to the idea the night before, but I had no fight left in me and I didn't want to take the chance of another argument. "For a walk, I need some air." I grabbed my cloak from the peg beside the door and hurried outside. Once there, I closed my eyes and pictured myself in front of Devin's home.

I had no idea if he'd even be there, but I had to start my search for him somewhere. Steeling myself, I walked up to the door and knocked on it. His mother opened it.

"What are you doing here?" she asked.

"I need to speak to Devin. Is he home?"

"You should not be here," she hissed.

"Please, Kileena." I took another step forward, and looked over her shoulder hoping for a glimpse of Devin.

"Listen to me, Lilli. You are a beautiful girl, and I can see why my son fell in love with you. But you are no good for him. He should have known better than to think the two of you had a future together. It was one thing when the both of you assumed you were half-human, but he should've walked away after the two of you learned Zoran was your father. Do you know how he will pay for his foolishness? With his life."

"I didn't plan for any of this to happen."

"But it did, and nothing can change that," she said. "You did as I asked and broke Devin's heart to save his life. For that I will always be grateful to you, but he won't survive having his heart broken like that again, which means you must stay away from him."

"You don't understand." I stopped myself before launching into an explanation. Kileena probably didn't know about Devin's involvement with the Resistance. He wouldn't have told her because she would've tried to stop him.

"What don't I understand?"

"Nothing," I said, backing away. "It was stupid of me to come here. I'm sorry."

I turned and ran, slowing down only after I'd put a good amount of distance between myself and Devin's home. I was still as determined as ever to find him, but I had no idea how. I couldn't show up at his door again, not after his mother's reaction to me.

I kept walking, hoping something would occur to me. The forest was quiet, like it always was. The only sounds came from rustling leaves and the occasional bird call. But suddenly I got a feeling that I was being followed. I stopped walking and listened for crunching leaves or snapping twigs underfoot. I heard nothing, except for the drumming of my heart. I looked over my shoulder and spotted someone off in the distance. At least it wasn't Zoran; his hair was darker and longer.

"Who's there?" I called out.

Slowly the man took a few steps closer, and though he was a good distance away, my heart leapt as I realized who it was.

"What have I told you about walking through the woods all by yourself?" he called out as he walked toward me.

"How long have you been following me?"

"Who said I was?" Devin stood only a few feet away from me now.

"Nobody." I shrugged my shoulders. "I just assumed."

"Are you afraid of me now?"

"Afraid?" I frowned. "Why would I be?"

"I can hear your heart beating like a drum. The only time it ever does that is when you're scared . . . or when you're excited to see me. But that can't be it."

Seeing him standing in front of me had tied my tongue. Several times I opened my mouth to say something, but I just couldn't find the right words.

"Why were you looking for me earlier?"

"How did you know I was? Your mother told me you weren't home."

"I wasn't," he said, his eyes sparkling as he stared into mine. "At least not when you first arrived. I came later and overheard you and my mother talking."

"So you decided to follow me?"

"Only to ask what you wanted."

Things between us were so awkward now that I had a hard time finding the right words. "There's something I need to talk to you about."

"That much I gathered," he said. "But does your new lover know you're out searching for me? Or does leaving a trail of broken hearts not bother you?"

"Kees isn't my lover. He never has been."

Devin laughed. "Do I look stupid? I've seen the two of you together, not just on the beach either, but at Tabitha's and walking around the Markets, holding hands." He gritted his teeth. "Always holding hands."

"It was only for show," I said, my heart pounding in anticipation of Devin's reaction to my confession. "To make you think Kees and I were together and that I didn't love you."

Devin took a step closer. His eyes narrowed as he stared at me. "What game are you playing, Lilli?"

I turned around, unable to look Devin in the eyes, and crossed my arms. "Zoran told me more than once that if I didn't end things with you, he'd kill you. I . . . I wanted to believe it was all talk, that he was too busy figuring out how to stay hidden from the Council to bother with what I was doing, but Rayden and my mother warned me that I was putting your life in danger. They told me I needed to convince you it was truly over if I wanted to keep you safe." A sudden chill ran through me, and I shivered. Devin inched toward me, removed his jacket, and draped it over my shoulders even though I already had a cloak on. "So that's what I did. And Kees helped me because he felt like he owed me after what happened in the Void. But it was all for nothing, hurting you. I thought I was saving your life, but I was wrong, wasn't I?" I turned to face Devin.

"Why couldn't you have told me any of this before?"

"Because Zoran would've found out somehow. He watches

me. Everything I say or do, I risk him finding out about."

"So why are you telling me this now?"

"There is no defeating Zoran. He's too strong. If you would have kept quiet and did as he told you to, there's a chance he would've spared your life, but instead you've gone and joined the Resistance. As soon as Zoran finds out you're opposing him—and he will find out—your life is as good as over," I said. "Which means I broke your heart, and mine, for nothing."

"Silly woman. Don't you know that a life without you in it, isn't worth living?" He reached for my hand, and I trembled at his touch.

I shook my head. "You're wrong."

Devin put his hand on my chin, lifting it, so I could meet his gaze. "Are you saying you still love me?"

"I never stopped. And I never will."

He closed his eyes briefly. "When you told me you didn't want to be with me, I felt like I'd died inside."

"I'm sorry for hurting you. But I hurt, too. Every second away from you was torture. The only thing that kept me going was the hope that I could get Zoran to trust me enough that he might reveal some weakness, some way to stop him. But he's too powerful. There is no stopping him, nor much time before he puts his plan into action. But whatever time is left, I want to spend it with you."

Devin's eyes brightened. Then he kissed me. It was the kind of kiss you give someone you're desperately afraid you'll never see again. The kind that rocks you to your core and makes you feel like the world is spinning. Having his lips on mine, his arms wrapped around me, was all I wanted. Even if it could only be for a short time, it was better than not having him at all.

"I feel like I can finally breathe again." Devin put his hands on the sides of my head and stared at me. "I can't believe you're really here. I can't believe I got to kiss you again. I was worried about that you know, that I'd die without getting the pleasure of kissing you at least once more."

"We don't have much time, Devin. For all I know Zoran could be watching us right now."

"I'm a dead man either way."

"Please don't say that," I said miserably.

"Kiss me again," he whispered, wrapping his fingers through my hair and pulling me closer. His lips parted mine as he pressed against me. I took a step backward, then another until the tree behind me stopped me from going any further. Devin reached for my hands, twining his fingers with mine as his lips traveled down the length of my neck. "I've missed you, Lilli. No matter how hard I tried, I couldn't stop thinking about you."

"I want to be with you," I breathed. "Even if it's our last time."

"I want that, too." Devin smiled. "And I know the perfect place."

He wrapped his arms around me, and a moment later I felt the two of us drifting. I had no idea where he was taking me, and I didn't care. Only one thing mattered—we were together.

"Open your eyes," he prompted after that strange floating sensation teleporting brought with it had eased.

When I did, I saw that we were in a small cabin. There was a bed wedged into the corner and an empty fireplace in another. There was also a table with four chairs, all of which had been turned over, and broken dishes on the floor.

My eyebrows furrowed in confusion. "What is this place?"

"This was meant to be our home one day. I built it anyway even after you told me you didn't want me anymore. I couldn't bring myself not to. I know it's not very big, and it's also pretty messy. After what happened at Tabitha's, I came here and in a fit of anger broke almost everything in sight."

"I don't care how big it is, or that it's not perfectly in order," I said turning around to get a better look. "This is our home, and for now we're together in it, that's all that really matters to me."

Devin lifted the overturned table back onto its legs. Then he did the same with the chairs, pushing them underneath. With his foot he kicked the broken pieces of porcelain out of the way.

"Wait," I said. "Let me."

I lifted my hands and spoke the words of a spell I'd been practicing. The debris on the floor quivered first before moving into a pile in the corner of the room.

"There," I said, satisfied with myself. I'd been getting better and better at magic.

"I'm impressed," Devin said, reaching for my hand and pulling me closer. His warm hand reached around the nape of my neck as he kissed me.

Kissing and stroking each other, we made our way over to the corner of the room and flopped down onto the bed. I ignored the ache in my heart as I realized that this bed was where Devin and I had been meant to be together for the first time as husband and wife one day. But we'd never get the chance to exchange vows. I told myself it didn't matter. I was Devin's wife in every way that mattered. He was my one and only, my forever.

"I love you," Devin whispered in my ear as he reached for the hem of my tunic.

I wrapped my arms around his broad back and, before locking my mouth on his hungrily, said, "I love you, too."

Chapter 26

I hadn't intended to fall asleep after, but snuggled in the crook of Devin's arms, I was so content that I drifted off while we were still in the middle of talking.

When I woke up, it was to the sound of my mother's voice. It was dark, too dark to see anything, so it took me a moment to realize her voice wasn't coming from anywhere nearby. She was speaking to me telepathically.

Lilli, please answer me. Where are you?

I'm with Devin.

And where are the two of you?

At our home. He built one for us.

You scared me and Rayden half to death. We haven't heard from you for hours.

I'm sorry. But I was afraid if I told either of you where I was going you'd try and talk me out of it.

Don't do that again. We were afraid something happened to you. When will you return home?

I'm not sure.

Okay, just do me a favor and be careful.

It was the middle of the night. Surely even my evil, powerful father had to sleep. Which meant Devin and I were safe, for now.

I turned on my side and put my arm over Devin's bare chest. He opened his eyes. "You're awake," he said.

"Yeah. My mother was worried. Didn't know where I was."

"I still can't believe you're really here."

"I never want to leave," I said. "I want to stay here with you for as long as I can."

"So you really don't think the Council has a chance of stopping Zoran?"

I shook my head. "He took me to the Underworld to show me the army ready to fight for him. He's got hundreds, maybe thousands, of gargoyles, and as far as I know they're indestructible," I said, explaining about the shield spell.

"I'm not afraid," he said, kissing the top of my head. "And I don't believe his gargoyles are truly indestructible. Everything and everyone has a weakness."

I wasn't afraid either, I realized as I closed my eyes. I fell back asleep easily, happy and content in Devin's arms.

Morning came faster than I wanted it to. I woke up to find Devin already out of bed.

"I made you breakfast," he said as I sat up.

"How did you manage to do that?"

"I snuck home while you were still sleeping and grabbed a few things."

I pulled back the covers, got out of bed, and hastily threw my clothes on. A basket of bread sat on the table, and I could smell eggs frying. Neither of us had dinner the night before, so I was starving. "It's a good thing your mother didn't catch you raiding her shelves," I said. "You know she hates me, right?"

"It isn't really you she hates, it's the situation."

"Devin, what if the two of us ran away and went back to the human world? If we're super careful, no one there ever has to find out we're witches."

"You think I haven't thought of that? But Zoran would eventually track us down wherever we went."

"What if we faked our deaths?" I asked, grasping for straws.

"I don't know, Lilli. Something like that seems awfully tricky to set up, given the short amount of time we have left. Your father is no fool." Devin sighed. "I hate that he's going to win and get whatever he wants."

"He's not, though. Zoran wants to be loved, but no one does. The Council cared for him once, but he went and messed that up. How empty of a life that must be. Truth is, a part of me feels sorry for him."

"I hate him too much to feel pity," Devin said. "I hate him for taking you from me, for what he did to you in the Void, and for what he's doing to the Wilds. Despite people's prejudices, I've always loved this place, but it's not the same anymore, and Zoran hasn't even won yet."

"And I hate that he's my father," I said, looking away, feeling disgusted that his blood ran through my veins.

"Hey." Devin put his hand on my cheek, forcing me to meet his gaze. "I've told you this before. You're nothing like him."

For a moment neither of us spoke. Then Devin leaned in and kissed me. When he pulled away he looked at me with a silly grin on his face and said, "Come on and eat before your breakfast gets cold."

I shook my head, laughing. Devin was always good at making me smile at the oddest times.

Just as I finished two eggs and a few slices of buttered bread, someone started banging loudly on the front door. For a moment my heart froze until it occurred to me that if it was Zoran, he wouldn't need to use a door to get inside. Whatever spell witches put on their homes to keep people from teleporting in uninvited didn't seem to affect him.

"Devin, I know you're in there. Open the door, please."

"What is your mother doing here?" I asked.

"I don't know," he replied. When his mother knocked again, more loudly this time, he went to open it.

Kileena hurried inside, followed by my mother and Rayden.

"I'm so sorry," my mother said. "I know you two wanted to be left alone, but Kileena was out of her mind with worry. I had to tell her what I knew."

"It's okay," I said, feeling bad that I hadn't even bothered to consider Kileena's feelings.

"Devin, I can't believe you'd be this reckless," Kileena said.

"So this is the place you were telling me about?" Rayden clapped Devin on the back. "It's a bit cozy, wouldn't you say?"

"I like cozy," I said.

"Bringing her here was a bad idea, Devin. Why can't you get it through your head that this girl," Kileena pointed at me, "will be the death of you?"

"I'm a dead man no matter what I do. Wouldn't you rather I spent my last days happy?"

My mother groaned. "Can we stop all this death talk?"

"You're married to Zoran," Kileena said, her hands clenched

together in front of her. "You know him better than any of us. Do you see this playing out any other way?"

"I . . . I don't really know," my mother stammered, once more giving me the feeling that there was something she was not telling us.

"I agree with Devin," Rayden said. "It's time we faced reality. Zoran has had weeks to prepare an army that magic and weapons cannot defeat. We have two choices. Let him have his victory or die fighting against him. I don't think there's any question which side all of us here will take. If our days are numbered, I'd rather spend them happily."

Kileena walked over to the table and sank into one of the chairs beside it. "I suppose you're right." She lifted her head and looked at me. "Tell us what you know. How much time do you think we have?"

"I don't really know. Zoran didn't really give me a timetable," I explained. "All he said was that he wanted to prove himself to me and my mother first. That a victory without us beside him was meaningless."

"Ina's death was a warning," Devin said. "Whatever is coming will be here soon."

"Perhaps we're thinking about this in the wrong way," Rayden said. "Relying on magic to defeat Zoran is a mistake. If we had weapons, human weapons, then maybe that army of Zoran's could be defeated."

I shook my head. "I doubt it. Besides, getting our hands on the kinds of weapons we'd need isn't exactly an easy thing to do."

Rayden sighed. "So much for that idea."

I was about to reply when I noticed that something had

gotten Devin's attention. He looked from side to side. "Do you all hear that?"

"Hear what?" his mother asked, her brow furrowed.

"Footsteps."

The rest of us looked at each other quizzically. Devin walked over to a window. I followed. My heart almost stopped at the sight of my father's gargoyles approaching. The sound of their footsteps growing louder as they came closer. Their stone like bodies made each movement sound like thunder. How had Zoran found me, and what did he mean to do?

"Those are the gargoyles I told you about," I said as my mother looked over my shoulder. "But there's supposed to be more of them. Lots more."

"Zoran has probably dispatched the rest to the Council's compound," my mother said. I glanced at her noticing that her face had gone pale.

"So this is it?" Kileena said.

"I wonder where Zoran is?" Rayden said.

Devin grasped my hand and clenched it tightly. "He's here."

I nearly screamed as I turned my head to find my father standing only a few feet away with a vicious smirk on his face.

Zoran crossed his arms. "What do we have here? A family get-together? Why wasn't I invited?"

My hands shook from a mixture of fear and anger. "What are you doing here?"

His eyes blazed. "Finding out why my daughter has defied me."

"Zoran, calm down." My mother walked over to him and put her hand on his arm. "Just because you do not approve of Devin, does not mean that he and Lilli cannot at least be friends."

"Do you really think I am that stupid?" Zoran said, fury warping his face. "Do you?"

"Of course not . . ."

"For eighteen years, you played me for a fool, Naiara. No more. You and Lilli are mine. And if I can't get the two of you to see that on your own, then you leave me with no other choice."

"People are not property," I protested.

"How wrong you are my child." An eerie smile spread across my father's face. "How wrong you are."

Chapter 27

Something about the way Zoran said those words set my teeth on edge.

"Why did you bring those creatures here?"

"As protection in case your mother decides to try something foolish like summoning for help."

"I wouldn't," she said.

"As you can see it would be futile," he said before turning his attention away from my mother to address all of us. "You are about to witness my power, but not all of you will live to warn others about it." We all stood frozen and mute while Zoran spoke. "One of you will die. Can any of you guess who?"

No one answered.

Zoran rolled his eyes. "How boring you all are," he said. "I guess that leaves it up to me to get the fun started."

"Kileena, your son will be the one to lose his life—and you will be the one taking it."

"You're an evil piece of filth," she hissed. "I would never hurt my son."

"Actually, you will do exactly as I tell you to."

Zoran, who was standing in the middle of the room turned his head from side to side to get a quick look at us all.

"I'm not afraid of you," Kileena said.

Zoran stared into Kileena's sea-green eyes. "Create fire," he commanded her.

A stunned look crossed her face. She lifted her hand. A moment later, a ball of fire formed in her palm. She stared at it, mesmerized.

"You elementals are such useful creatures. Too bad I didn't create an army with your talents. Imagine the power."

"What are you doing to her?" Devin said, his voice full of anger as he looked at his mother and saw the panic in her eyes.

Kileena seemed to be in some sort of trance. The ball of fire she'd just created hovered several inches above her palm. She gazed at it curiously, like she had no idea how it had gotten there.

"Kill him," Zoran commanded, pointing to Devin.

"No!" I exclaimed. Panic spread through me as I realized what Zoran was doing. "Don't do it. Devin is your son and he loves you. Whatever Zoran is doing to your mind, you have to fight it," I pleaded with Kileena.

"He's my son, and I love him," she said, but lifted her hand anyway as if readying herself to fling that ball of fire in her son's direction.

I reached deep into my mind, plucking out the most loving memories I had. Kate and the man who raised me, the man I'd called Dad, hugging me after graduation. His kisses before I went to bed. The way he'd comforted me every time I had a bad dream. I cast them out over everyone in the room, too panicked to focus only on Kileena.

She smiled and lowered her hand.

Zoran spun to face me. "You're not strong enough to stop me. And know this, soon you'll be under my command the same way the half-breed's mother is."

"You can't do this. Not even you could be this evil. You cannot make a mother kill her own child."

"Oh, but I can. I can do whatever I want, and the sooner you and everyone else realizes that, the less tedious my life will become." Zoran turned back around. "Listen to me," he said to Kileena. "The half-breed must die, and you must be the one to make that happen."

"He must die," Kileena said.

"Mother, no."

Kileena lifted her hand once more. This time she hurled the ball of fire at her son. He managed to duck. The flames struck the wall leaving a charred hole behind.

"He must die," Kileena said again. More flames formed in her hand. Rayden tried to reach her but she moved too quickly, once more hurling another fireball at Devin.

"No," I cried out, realizing that Kileena wouldn't stop her pursuit until she succeeded in carrying out Zoran's command.

For the second time, Kileena missed Devin.

Zoran laughed. "This is too much fun. But it's taking too long. Perhaps she needs a little help. What do you people think?"

As Kileena let go of one more ball of flames, Zoran guided it telekinetically. Devin was too far away from me for me to throw myself in front of him, but my mother wasn't. She intercepted the ball of fire before it reached Devin. As she jumped in front of him her clothes caught fire. She screamed in pain as the fire quickly spread, burning her.

"No!" Zoran shouted and lunged for my mother who had collapsed to the floor. "How foolish can you be, Naiara?" He pounded at the fire on her clothing quickly putting it out, but he hadn't been fast enough. My mother just lay there, limp in his arms. Zoran turned his head and shouted at Rayden. "You're supposed to be a healer. Don't just stand there, do something."

It was as if his command awakened both Rayden and I who were standing there in shock. As Rayden ran over to help, I ran over with something entirely different on my mind. A rage I'd never felt before took over guiding me to reach for the dagger sheathed around my calf. I pulled it out. With my father's back turned to me as he crouched down beside my mother, begging her to be okay, I realized I had the perfect opportunity.

Before I truly thought through what I was doing, I plunged the dagger straight into my own father's back. His body went perfectly still. I pulled the dagger out and plunged it in once more like a madwoman. And then I froze. Blood dripped from the blade I had just pulled out of Zoran's back for the second time.

He turned around slowly to face me, his face already losing its color. "What have you done?"

I threw the dagger onto the ground and turned away from my mother who was covered in burns and my father who was bleeding to death. Then, unable to hold myself upright a second longer, I sank to my knees, covering my face with my hands.

Time seemed to stop. I had no idea how much of it passed before Devin knelt beside me and wrapped his arm around my shoulders. "It's over," he whispered into my ear.

Chapter 28

Slowly, Devin eased me up off the floor. The ground beneath me shook. A loud rumbling came from outside.

"What's happening?"

"Take a look," Devin said.

With wobbly feet I took a few steps toward the window closest to me and sucked in a breath at the sight of what was happening outside. The gargoyles Zoran had brought with him were breaking into pieces leaving nothing but large chunks of stone behind. I knew what that meant and turned my head back around to look at my father who lay a few feet away from me flat on his back. Blood oozed from his mouth and scorch marks covered his chest. Kileena, who was standing right beside his body, must've finished the job for me.

Rayden was on his knees beside my mother running his hands over her burned body and uttering some sort of spell.

"Can you heal her?" I asked, praying with everything in me that his answer would be yes.

"He needs to focus, Lilli. Let him be," Devin whispered.

I turned and buried my head in his chest, unable to look at

the scene in front of me for even one second more. "I can't believe I just killed my own father."

Devin reached for my still shaking hands and pulled me away so he could look into my eyes. "You saved my life. And more than that, you saved the lives of every person who would've dared take a stand against Zoran. What you did was brave."

I shook my head. "I don't feel very brave." It had been anger, anger and opportunity that made me attack my father.

"Lilli." Rayden called me over. He was still kneeling beside my mother holding one of her hands. "I need you to come over here."

I dashed over and reached for my mother's other hand. Her eyes were closed. Burns and ash stained her beautiful porcelain skin.

"Lilli," she said in a weak voice.

"Don't talk, mother. Save your strength."

"Is he okay?" she asked.

"Is who okay?"

"Devin."

All of a sudden, the sacrifice my mother had just made struck me. I bit my lip and swallowed the lump in my throat before reaching out to brush my mother's hair with my hand. "He's fine. Thanks to you."

"Naiara. You need to save your strength," Rayden said. "No more talking for now."

"Will she be all right?" I asked.

Rayden nodded. "I think so. But she isn't fully recovered. I should take her home so she can continue to recuperate."

"I need a word with Naiara before you leave," Kileena said.

She turned away from Zoran's body. I eased my hand free from my mother's and walked back over to Devin's side.

"You saved my son's life," Kileena said to my mother after kneeling down beside her. "I am in debt to you."

"The only payment I ask is that you give Devin and Lilli your blessing. They love each other so much."

Kileena turned her head to look at us. "They've always had it. I knew from the moment I met your daughter that she was a special person."

My mother smiled. "She really is." My mother started coughing, and then closed her eyes tightly, grimacing.

Rayden took my mother's hand again. A moment later the two of them vanished leaving Devin, his mother and me behind in the cabin along with my father's dead body.

"We need to let the Council know what has happened," Devin said.

He still wore the amulet we'd been given by Lina, which he grasped in his hand before reciting the incantation we'd been taught. A moment later, there was a knock on the door. Kileena opened it and let two cloaked figures inside. The Messengers drew back their hoods and surveyed the scene. I didn't recognize either of them.

"Tell me what happened," one of them said, his gaze fixed on Zoran's body.

Thankfully, Devin spoke first and explained what had taken place. After he described the way my mother had jumped in front of him to save his life, he stopped talking, too afraid to tell anyone what I'd done. But I knew they'd only keep asking questions until everything was out in the open.

"While Zoran was distracted by my mother's injuries I stabbed him in his back."

"And I finished him off," Kileena added.

"It is with great sadness that I offer my gratitude to the two of you for ending his life. Never would I have imagined being grateful for the death of the boy I and the rest of the Messengers and Council loved as if he were our child," one of the Messengers said.

"Do you have any other questions?" I asked.

"Nothing for now."

"Thank you." I didn't think I had it in me to answer any more questions. I was exhausted, still in shock over what I'd done, and worried about my mother.

I turned to Devin and took his hands. "Take your mother home."

"I want to be with you."

"And you will be," I said. "But not until you've taken care of your mother first."

Devin kissed my forehead. "I love you," he said.

"I love you, too." I closed my eyes and a moment later I found myself back home.

I very badly wanted to see my mother, but Rayden asked me to wait. "She's still healing. She needs her rest, and so do you."

He walked over to me with a cup of tea in his hands. I barely drank half of it before I became overwhelmed with a deep need for sleep. Rayden had put some sort of sedative in my drink. I remembered him helping me to my bedroom, but nothing more, for I fell into a dark and dreamless sleep.

Chapter 29

When I woke up, Devin was seated beside me on the bed.

"Hello, beautiful."

The sky outside was already starting to darken. "How long have I been sleeping?"

"For most of the day," Devin replied. "Which I'm happy about. You needed the rest."

The morning's events came back to me in a sudden rush. "How is my mother doing? Is she all right?"

"She is still recovering, but Rayden said she is much better. He's managed to heal her internal injuries. Her burns will take a bit longer."

I sat up. "I want to see her."

"She's in your cousin's room."

I threw back the covers and darted out of my bedroom and into Rayden's. My mother looked so much better than she had earlier. As I sat beside her she opened her eyes. "Lilli," she said.

"Why did you do it?" I asked. "Why did you jump in front of Devin?"

"I told you once that a mother would do anything for her child."

"You could have died."

"I would have gladly given my life to preserve your happiness."

I stared down at her, feeling more love for her than I'd ever imagined I could, and more shame than I cared to admit for not realizing before how much she had sacrificed for me. "I was so angry with you for walking out on me and Dad. Even after you explained why you did it, I couldn't bring myself to truly forgive. But now I get it. I'm sorry for how harshly I judged you."

"Don't be sorry. You have no need to be."

"You told me once that the reason you didn't kill Zoran and instead endured being his wife was because you knew it would change you—"

"Don't," she said, realizing where my mind had taken me. "You didn't plan to kill Zoran, it happened in the heat of the moment. And the Zoran you killed was far worse than the one I lived with while you were still a child. That Zoran hadn't been completely taken over by darkness yet."

"I just can't believe it, though," I said, staring down at my hands. The ones I'd used to take a life.

"Life sometimes demands hard choices. You made the right one." My mother reached for one of my hands, wincing from the pain the movement caused. I moved closer to her.

"When you jumped in front of Devin, did you know this would happen? Did you know that your injuries would provide the distraction needed for me to end Zoran's life?"

"No. I didn't see as far as that. All I knew was that Zoran would use Devin's own mother to try to end his life and that I'd be the one to save him. That's as far as my vision went."

So that's what she'd been keeping from me. I knew there was

something. Before I could ask her why she didn't tell me, there was a knock on the door. Rayden stuck his head in the room. "I don't mean to interrupt, but you have a visitor, Lilli."

I frowned. "Who is it?"

"Syre."

"Go," my mother said. "I know he isn't your favorite person, but you should hear him out."

I got up and followed Rayden to the living room, where Syre was standing, his commanding presence instantly making me feel smaller. Devin was there, too. He walked over to me and threaded his fingers through mine.

We approached Syre together, side by side. He bowed and said, "I owe you my life."

"It wasn't you I was thinking about when I stabbed my father in his back."

"But it is my life, along with many others, that you saved, which means I am indebted to you," he said. "If there is ever anything you need, you have only to ask."

"The only thing I need is my family." Devin loosened his hand from mine and put his arm around my shoulders pulling me closer to him. "And Devin."

"No one on the Council seeks to stand in the way of your happiness, Lilli. We have made mistakes in regards to you, but hurting you was never our intention."

"What happens now? Zoran might be dead, but what about the demons he's been plotting with and the rest of his gargoyles?"

"When a witch dies the spells he or she has cast break," Syre replied. "It's why I told you the only way to win was to kill Zoran."

When I'd seen those gargoyles crumble outside of Devin's window I'd suspected as much. Still, it was a relief to hear Syre confirm it. "So it's over then?"

Syre nodded. "I'm sorry that it had to be you. If I could've killed him, I would have, but I didn't stand a chance of getting close enough to him to succeed. I know nothing I say will erase the guilt you feel, but the fact that you feel guilt at all shows how different you and Zoran are from each other."

I stared at Syre. "I can think of a way you can repay me." Perhaps it was a long shot, but Syre had said that if I needed anything all I had to do was ask.

He stared back inquisitively.

"The people of the Wilds need leaders who will do more than protect them from dark magic. They need leaders that set an example. They need to be taught that regardless of how powerful of a witch you are, or what your family name is, that we are all equals. You told me once the Council doesn't involve itself in people's personal affairs. Maybe it's time you reconsider that position."

"A tall order."

"You can start by outlawing arranged marriages like the one my mother ran away from. People should be free to choose who to love."

"What you are asking for won't be easy. Not everyone will see things the way you do, and change takes time, dear child," he said.

"I realize that. But we have to start somewhere."

Syre walked back over to me and kissed me on my forehead. "I know you must still be angry with me. I understand if you are.

But I will say this, getting to know you has been one of the greatest privileges of my life."

He walked away after that, leaving Rayden, Devin and me alone, too stunned to really know what to say to each other.

"What do you think this all means?" I said after a while.

"I think it means that dream you once told me about will come true after all," Rayden said.

"Which dream was that?" Devin asked.

I reached for his hand, pulling him closer and kissing him. "The one where I was surrounded by my family," I said, then kissed him again before adding, "And you."

Devin smiled. His arms wrapped around my waist and he stared into my eyes. "It's not a dream anymore, Lilli. It's real. You and me, my family and yours joined. Everything that once stood in our way is gone."

My heart leapt. After everything we'd been through it was hard to believe, but Devin was right. It had been a long and bumpy road, but I'd finally found my happily ever after.

The End

Want to be notified when Teresa Roman's next book will be released? Then sign up for her mailing list by going to http://eepurl.com/bSYLZr. Your email address will never be shared and you can unsubscribe at any time.

Word of mouth and reviews are essential for an author's success. If you enjoyed this book, please consider leaving a review. Even a short review would be helpful and greatly appreciated.

Thank you.

Connect with me online.
Website: www.teresaromanwrites.com
Facebook: www.facebook.com/teresaromanauthor
Twitter: www.twitter.com/TRomanauthor
Goodreads:
www.goodreads.com/author/show/14163515.Teresa_Roman
Instagram: www.instagram.com/teresaromanauthor/

Also by Teresa Roman:

Back to Us
Out of Nowhere
Daughter of Magic
Legacy

Acknowledgements

I want to start by thanking my readers. There are literally millions of books out there and I'm honored that you chose to read mine. I would also like to thank my family, especially my little sister and my children. For months my middle child has been asking when this book will finally be ready. It amazes me that my daughter loves my books so much, and I am beyond flattered by her praise. A big thank you also goes out to my amazing editor, Linda Cassidy Lewis, who is more than just a fabulous editor, but an amazing author as well. What a blessing it is to be able to write and share stories with the world. Thank you to everyone who has supported me on this journey.

About the Author

Teresa Roman writes contemporary and paranormal romance for adults and young adults. If it was possible to be born with a book in her hands, that's how Teresa Roman would've entered this world. Her passion for reading is what inspired her to become a writer. She loves the way stories can take you to another time and place.

Born in Romania, Teresa has lived in the Midwest and on both coasts, but currently calls Sacramento, CA, her home. She lives there with her husband, three adorable children, two cats, and a dog. When she's not at her day job or running around with her kids, you can find her in front of the computer writing, or with her head buried in another book.